Metamorphosis
and other
Short Stories

Metamorphosis
and other
Short Stories

J. Graham Ducker

First Edition

Hidden Brook Press
www.HiddenBrookPress.com
writers@HiddenBrookPress.com

Metamorphosis and other Short Stories
by Graham Ducker

Cover Photograph – Richard M. Grove
Cover Design – Richard M. Grove
Layout and Design – Richard M. Grove

Typeset in Garamond
Printed and bound in Canada
Distributed in USA by Ingram,
          in Canada by Hidden Brook Distribution

Library and Archives Canada Cataloguing in Publication

Title: Metamorphosis : and other short stories / J. Graham Ducker.
Other titles: Short stories. Selections
Names: Ducker, J. Graham, author.
Identifiers: Canadiana 20190088109 | ISBN 9781927725733 (softcover)
Classification: LCC PS8563.R31457 A6 2019 | DDC C813/.6—dc23

This book is dedicated to:

My wonderful wife, Stella,
who has encouraged me to keep writing.

My terrific grandson
who has inspired many stories.

All those who enjoy short stories,
some of which have an unexpected twist.

Richard Grove (Tai)
whose infinite patience and persistence
made this book possible.

Contents

Foreword

I think it was my Grandma Hall that initiated the idea of writing short stories. When I was about eight years old she gave me a six-volume set called *The Children's Hour*, which I relished reading. I still remember some of those stories.

I recall a rather thick, maroon, Grade seven English book, in which various short-story writers had different and often surprise endings.

I appreciate the conciseness of a short story which dispenses with a lot of the fluff and fill.

I also like giving inanimate things and/or nebulous concepts a voice, and developing plots through ethereal conversations.

Putting a new twist on the old fairy tales is fun.

Incorporating my protagonist, a twelve-year-old boy into various situations, gives rise to many unique episodes.

Occasionally, I like to leave the reader contemplating a possible continuation to the narrative.

Graham Ducker

Another Time, Another Place

A warm autumn breeze blew through the yard as the real estate agent and Jeremy relaxed on some old lawn chairs and contemplated the old farm house.

The uncut grass did its best to hide incomplete sections of a split-rail fence that marked off long-unused areas.

A sealed well sat beside the weather-beaten barn.

Large trees shaded the south side of the typical late nineteenth century farm house, built solidly square to withstand the rigours of time, friends and family.

The cedar-shingled roof was still in good shape.

Behind a white railing a wood-plank veranda crept around the house where main floor windows enjoyed the protection of the weathered covering.

Above this, bedroom windows peeked out between shutters, some of which dangled from one hinge.

The agent Harris patted the papers in his lap.

"There is still time to change your mind, you know."

"No," said Jeremy, "It is quite charming. This is exactly what I was looking for – something that might inspire a book."

The agent chuckled and pointed at the house. "Well, this place just might do the trick."

"I did think the price was a tad low for such gorgeous old building. Is there something I should know?"

The agent scratched his leg. "I hesitated to mention one aspect in case it scared you off."

Jeremy pointed towards town. "The old lady who owns the motel warned me that the place was haunted."

"Well, although things happened many years ago, there is always a basis to a persistent rumour."

Jeremy shrugged. "You can't stop people from talking. I think the folks around these parts have kept the story going just to have something to talk about."

The agent pressed on. "How do you explain the owner falling down and drowning in his own well?"

"It probably happened once in a while back in those days, I suppose. Thanks to your notes, I've read a bit of the history. The inquest was routine and its conclusions were, as far as I can tell, reasonable."

"It certainly divided the community"

"His wife must have been devastated."

"They say she wasn't."

Jeremy patted the agent's shoulder. "I would certainly like to meet this 'they' person who opines every thing that is not factual."

"But the man had powerful friends. Apparently they conspired to cheat the widow out of her inheritance. They surreptitiously bought the land and had her evicted."

"Where was her lawyer? He could have done something!"

"He was in on it. When the judge sided with the group, she put a curse on the farm."

"I don't blame her!"

"Ah, but what you don't know is that she also put one on the men."

"Good for her."

"And it was uncanny how each one died under strange circumstances."

"Spells can be powerful."

"Apparently the apparition that appears each time someone tries to buy the house. That's why people keep changing their minds."

"I'll be fine," Jeremy said. "Tell you what: if the spirit shows up, I'm sure there will be room for both of us."

Harry sighed and smiled as if a great weight had been removed from his shoulders.

The real estate agent stood up. As they shook hands the agent handed Jeremy a packet of papers.

"Okay then. I can't say I'm sorry to see it go. Here are the keys, although why it was locked up in the first place, I'll never know. I wish you all the best, although I won't be surprised if you show up back at my office."

"Thank you very much."

As the real estate agent's car disappeared, Jeremy plopped back into the ratty lawn chair and pondered the old house.

Well I wanted an adventure and it certainly appears as though I have bought a dandy.

His initial investigation showed the structure had a sound foundation. Paint and the small exterior repairs could wait while he puttered with the interior improvements.

Jeremy glanced at the height of the afternoon sun.

I might as well have another look inside while there is still some daylight. I'll ask Hydro to hook me up as soon as possible.

The veranda boards groaned as he walked to the door. The hinges whined as the heavy carved door swung back and thumped against the wall.

The foyer floor-boards also creaked.

My first job will be to dust these floors with talcum powder.

He absorbed the scene. *I'm in another time and space.*

The floor squeaked as he moved to his left. An imprinted door led into a study where a grand desk seemed to be waiting for some activity. Numerous shelves with various books framed a window which looked out over the treed landscape.

Opposite the study and behind antique sliding doors, a spacious living room sported an ornate old sofa and several worn arm chairs facing a huge stone fireplace.

Various side tables with antique lamps completed the scene.

In a huge ornate frame above the mantle was a portrait of a rather austere gentleman.

One of the first things I'm going to do is to get rid of that painting.

The floor boards continued to emit various sounds as he entered the hall and stood at the bottom of a large staircase.

He knew the hall to the left led back to the huge country kitchen and its pantry.

The staircase ascended to a landing where it jogged left up to the rooms upstairs.

Dominating the landing wall was the portrait of a beautiful lady in a gown with lace surrounding a squared décolletage. A gorgeous jewelled necklace sparkled below her delicate face.

She was smiling.

Her eyes were not.

I'm starting to imagine things.

Although the house was warm, Jeremy shivered.

He was about to go to the kitchen when a soft voice asked, "Do you like the place?"

Jeremy spun around to discover a demure tiny lady standing just inside the doorway.

He blinked. It was as if he had seen her before.

Although never being one to worry about fashion, he did notice that her outfit was a bit behind-the-times.

"I'm sorry. I don't mean to stare. My name is Jeremy Hudson." He stepped back. "Would you like to come in?"

"Yes, please. Thank you. I'm Emily."

Why don't the boards squeak when she walks on them? She's probably too light.

"Are you planning on living here?"

"Well, yes. I just bought it. I like to think I'm a writer, so I'm hoping it will inspire some creativity."

There was a twinge of caution in her tone.

"Yes, I quite like its atmosphere."

She stopped in the living room doorway and glared at the fireplace picture.

He followed her stare. "I'm going to throw that picture out. I don't fancy having him staring at me all day."

The tiny woman continued to stare.

Jeremy added, "He appears to have been a very controlling person."

"He was a pig."

Scrambling for words Jeremy managed, "Er, I wouldn't know."

"Everyone thought he was so wonderful the way he spread his money around."

"So he was a generous sort then?"

"Only when it suited his purpose. He was a dominating beast to me and the kids."

Jeremy wondered if she was even aware of him.

"I put up with his abuse for years. When Cindy, my eldest daughter, who was usually quite the chatterbox, suddenly became quiet, I knew something was wrong."

The woman turned and looked directly at Jeremy. "A mother knows her child.

"Of course."

"Cindy grew distant and insular. I tried to talk to her to find out what might be bothering her like problems at school, perhaps boys, you know, 'girl stuff''.

Jeremy nodded.

Deep hurt and anger blazed from the beautiful eyes.

"One day, after a get-together, I asked her to help with the dishes. She was very tense. She kept dropping the cutlery. I asked her if something was wrong. She said no. She knew I did not believe her. Then she dropped one of the good dishes which shattered all over the floor. When we knelt down to pick up the pieces, she started to cry. I hugged her and asked her what was wrong. She said nothing. I shook her shoulders. 'Something has you very upset. What is it? Tell me!' She said, 'I can't. He'll kill me.' 'Who?' Cindy wouldn't say. I yelled at her, 'WHO?' 'Dad!' My heart froze. Finally the truth finally came out. The pig had tried something with her but she escaped and ran out of the bedroom. I'm sure you know what I'm talking about. He threatened to kill her or me if she talked.

"So, that is why I killed him."

"Perfectly understandable. Everyone has limits. There is an old expression: 'Don't get between a mama bear and her cubs.'"

She faced Jeremy. "You understand."

"Yes I do. I've just finished an article about child abuse.

"You may stay."

As he looked at her, the lady slowly faded.

As Jeremy headed for the kitchen he looked up at the portrait on the landing.

The eyes were smiling.

Rescuing Rapunzel; or Not

Sir Paul the Persistent stumbled out of the thorny enchanted forest.

"I finally made it," he growled. "I certainly hope she's worth the effort. Rescuing Princesses are a pain in the butt. From all reports they become incessant nags."

He suppressed his bitterness. He was, after all, a Prince Charming.

Sir Paul hid to watch for the witch.

Just as he was about to remove an irritating thorn, a woman carrying a basket appeared.

The Prince blinked. Mentally prepared for the typical hideous hag, he was pleasantly surprised at the graceful figure.

As far as witches go she wasn't half bad.

A jaunty feathered hat covered brunette curls that fell around her shoulders. The delicate neck, cuddled by the violet cloak, inferred a matching body was secreted in the velvet folds. The tiny mole on her cheek was a bit distracting but other than that....

But why was she was wearing such heavy work gloves?

He dismissed these preliminary assessments. Right now, the quest was his priority.

The witch called, "Rapunzel! Rapunzel! Let down your hair."

A cascade of long dirty – perhaps blond – hair descended. The witch tightened her hat, hooked the basket in her elbow, grasped the tresses and hand-over-hand pulled herself up to the tiny balcony.

Her strength was amazing!

Eventually the woman reappeared at the railing.

"And keep this place cleaner," she admonished the hidden resident. "It would be good practise for you when your prince comes, if he ever does."

Her cackle continued as she slid to the ground whereupon she removed the gloves.

With her mantle swirling about her, the witch strode to the thorny wall which opened and enveloped her.

The hair-rope vanished upwards.

Sir Paul the Persistent allowed sufficient time to lapse before venturing out to stand beneath the parapet.

He made a controlled call. "Rapunzel! Rapunzel! Let down your hair."

When nothing happened he yelled, "Rapunzel! Rapunzel! Let down your hair!"

A rather unkempt girl peered down at him.

"Who's calling?"

The Prince waved. "It's me, your Prince Charming who has come to rescue you."

"Well, it's about time!"

"Sorry Miss Princess but I was delayed by...."

"Do you know how long I've been stuck up here?"

"Er, not really; I was just sent to...."

"Never mind! I'll throw down my hair so you can climb up. Meanwhile I'll pack."

A mass of hair tumbled down, but when Sir Paul pulled on it, the grimy locks slipped through his fingers. No matter how hard he squeezed he could not hold the oily tresses. Rubbing sand on his hands did not help.

"Now I know why the witch wore work gloves," he gritted.

The dishevelled woman's head reappeared.

"What's taking you so long? I haven't got all day you know."

Sir Paul snarled, "When was the last time you washed your hair?"

"I don't know. I can't remember. Every time I do it is a major chore. I hate it. I have to wait till the Witch brings some shampoo, and then haul up buckets of water all afternoon. It's no fun you know."

Sir Paul made a few more attempts, each one less enthusiastic than the last.

"Are you coming up or not?" cranked the voice.

Decisiveness edged the Prince's voice.

"I'm sorry Princess, but I am not strong enough to climb up there." He paused and then continued the lie. "I'll alert another Prince Charming who will be much stronger than I am."

Sir Paul grinned and muttered. "I'll send Sir Donald the Disgusting. The two of them will make a great fit."

Relief filled the Prince as he cajoled. "Please be patient a little while longer."

"Some hero you are," she snapped.

The head disappeared, quickly followed by the hair.

With shoulders set, the Prince strode to the spot where the witch had vanished.

He ran his fingers through his hair, straightened his tunic and shrugged.

"Well, I've come this far: nothing ventured — nothing gained."

With visions of the comely cloaked form, Sir Paul the Persistent faced the forest and smiled.

The branches opened and gently enfolded him.

Chez Pierre

"Hey, guess what?" I said, interrupting my wife in the middle of some intricate sewing, "I have been given a week off. Maybe we could get away somewhere."

She didn't miss a stitch. "And just where is 'somewhere'?"

"Oh, I don't know…" – I knew she did not like unplanned excursions – "…just away."

"Away."

She had an irritating way of repeating what I said, which forced further explanation. r.

"Well, you know, away, away from…" I motioned my hand around the room. "…from this."

"This."

She did it again!

"Yeah," I hurried on, "You know, away to some quiet little place."

"It's quiet here."

"I know dear, but a quiet place like," – I knew I was on dangerous ground – "like Pierre's cabin. Remember he said we could use it at any time."

I hovered.

"His cabin."

Good, she was coming around.

"Yeah! Apparently it's a lovely little spot. No TV, no radio.

"No water."

"No telephone."

"No lights."

"No noisy neighbours," I added but I was losing the battle.

Her eyes blazed. "You think I'm crazy!"

She was gorgeous when she was angry.

"Gosh, no, Honey! It's just that it would be *different*. It might be *fun*"

I emphasized the 'fun' part.

"Look," she stated in a tone that was calm and dead level, which usually denoted some impending disaster, — I was determined to ignore it — "If you really want to turn pioneer for a week, here's what we will do. We will find the camping equipment, and *we* will organize the supplies, and *we* will pack the truck."

My mind raced ahead. '*Wow, we are going!*'

"And *you* will go for the week."

The statement had finality.

"But I thought that we…"

"There is no 'we' here."

"But…"

"Look," she smiled and patted my cheek, "You go and have your quiet week at Pierre's cabin. You have been dying to get there for ages and you can fish and canoe to your heart's content."

"But what about you?"

"I will be fine. I have a few projects in mind, and it will be great to get at them without having you hanging around my neck."

"Then I'll nip over to Pierre's."

As my neighbour handed me his sketch of haphazard logging roads, one of which led to his cabin, he cautioned, "Better take lots of mosquito coils."

Other than that last ominous note, I was excited and spent the rest of the day organizing.

It was somewhat disconcerting that, when I kissed my wife goodbye, she did not have   that I'll-miss-you look.

After many hours of scrambling around miles of old neglected logging roads, I finally found the one that led to a little lake where a rustic cabin had CHEZ PIERRE painted above the door.

The interior was soon feeling cozy with the wood-burning stove was spreading its warmth around the room. The acrid tendrils from several mosquito coils added to the camping atmosphere. As I laid out the sleeping bag on the iron bed-springs I knew it was going to be a lumpy night, but I was too tired to care.

I was looking forward to the morning.

As it turned out, finding the cabin was the easy part. Between sawing and chopping wood, fetching water, cooking and cleaning amid the constant battle with mosquitoes, black flies and sand flies, survival became paramount. Running the gauntlet to the outhouse where mosquitoes ambushed my more tender parts me just added to the 'fun'.

It was a pleasure to get to bed each night.

It was a long week.

Actually the last two days were not too bad, but home began to look more appealing.

"Has it been a week already?" grinned my wife in mock surprise when I almost fell into the kitchen.

"Feels like a month!"

"I hope you had lots of fun, dear," she teased.

"Oh yeah, lots of fun."

She looked extremely well rested.

For an instant I hated her.

I headed for the hall.

"I'm going to take a long hot bath and shave. I'll unpack the truck later – tomorrow – sometime – maybe."

"That's fine, dear," she called after me. "Supper will be ready in when you come down."

"Wonderful," I mumbled. "What are we having?"

"Fish!"

Her peals of laughter chased me upstairs.

Upon arriving in the kitchen I discovered she had had one of her marvellous stews simmering on the stove.

During supper I happened to look across the table at her and saw a rather thoughtful look on her face. I could not help wondering if she was planning to have me to go back again next year.

A Hollow Hint

Cathy's Grandma fumed in the kitchen. Her anger gave impetus to her stirring the cream puff batter.

"That stupid Grand-daughter of mine has gone out with that dolt Jeffrey again! I don't know what she sees in such an empty-headed character. There is nothing there! Oh sure, he may be cute and well-dressed and all, but there is more to a relationship than a giggle. She doesn't heed her mom and she certainly won't listen to me. How can I get through to her stubborn mind? I'd have to hit over the head with a two by...."

As she reached for the cookie sheet, a grin began.

Later that evening – but earlier than usual – Cathy returned from her date, threw her purse and shoes into the corner, and then leaned back against the door.

"That Jeffrey is so...so...."

Exact words eluded her.

The aroma of fresh baking penetrated her mood. Cathy hurried to the kitchen to find four cupcakes beckoning from a plate on the table.

With a glass of milk in hand she closed her eyes and bit into a puff.

It shattered.

It was hollow.

She thought of Jeffrey.

"Thanks Grandma."

Colourful Thoughts

Jeremy quietly seethed.

"Stupid teacher! I don't have a favourite colour! How can I write about my favourite colour if I don't have one? Colours mean different things at different times. I hate Grade Four."

Jeremy glared at his notebook where the words: My favourite colour is – had been written a 'dog's-age' ago.

The other kids were busily working around him.

He dumped out his box of eight crayons and lined them up across his desk.

The black was neat and reminded him of the eyes of the squirrels he fed at the park, but it sure wasn't his 'favourite'. He put it into the box.

The red was next, and while he rolled it in his fingers, he thought of robins, strawberries, and apples; then recalled his bloody hands when he went for that tumble.

'Stupid bicycle,' he thought as he stuffed the crayon in the box.

He fingered the brown one. His lip trembled as he remembered his wonderful old dog Merlin that was run over last year. Jeremy slowly slid that colour out of sight.

The green one made him think of grass and leaves and

playing in the moss. It also reminded him of broccoli and asparagus and Brussels sprouts. There were lots of reasons for not liking green. The green joined the others.

Next, he picked up the orange one because it instantly reminded him of oranges, cheese, pumpkin pie and Mom's Kraft Dinner. Suddenly he shivered, as he could almost taste the squash his Mom tried to get him to eat last night. The orange crayon vanished.

The blue crayon gave him visions of summer skies and swimming at the beach. As he shifted in his desk, the desk thumped his left arm right where he had fallen on the boulder yesterday. He looked at the huge bruise, which was an ugly mixture of blues and purples. He thought of grapes and plums as the purple joined the blue in the box.

Only the yellow remained. Jeremy smiled as thoughts of bananas, buttercups, the summer sun, and – glancing across to his left – the blond girl who was two rows over and two seats up.

Jeremy picked up his pencil. He could talk about yellow but he would not mention Mary Ann.

Robert Bluette –
Pioneer of the
Automated Farm

Count Robert Louis Bluette De Blumenord was born on May 16, 1745 to Le Marquis Jacques De Bluette, a wealthy and powerful landowner.

King Louis XIV, the Sun King, established the original estate for the many years of loyal service by the Bourbon-Vendômes family. The lands and rolling hills around the city of Blumenord – known today as Villedieu les Poele in south western Normandy – were ceded in 1702 to the Marquis' family. The King also created the distinctive name Bluette to signify the special designation of the region.

After a succession of five daughters Robert, the son and heir, was joyfully welcomed as the estate's continuity was assured.

Small and sickly for much of his early years, Robert was utterly spoiled by his parents and his five sisters. It is thought that this pampering contributed to his complete lack of responsibility and disdainful attitude towards possessions. Even the philosopher Rene Descartes, in one of his many dissertations, briefly alluded to this correlation.

Robert Bluette De Blumenord was always dressed in blue.

The Marquise, Madam Charlotte, spared no expense and imported the finest of materials from which to make the lad's clothes.

It was ascertained that Robert was a clever creative child who was a voracious reader. His private tutors found it difficult to keep him interested as Robert quickly grasped any new concepts presented to him.

Initial scrutiny often deemed Robert as lazy, however this notion was quickly allayed after it was observed that he excelled in finding unique simple methods to do menial time-consuming tasks.

Despite his heritage, the child showed little interest in wealth or prominence. Much to his Mother's — and especially the father's — chagrin, the boy spent most of his free time in the surrounding fiefs where the country folk treated him kindly and willingly instructed him in the care and maintenance of livestock.

On his twenty-first birthday day his parents asked if he wanted anything in particular. He surprised everyone by announcing that he wanted to have a little farm of his own, where he could keep some sheep, a couple of cows, a few chickens, and maybe a pig or two. He also stated he wanted two special black and white dogs and a horn.

Robert was decidedly evasive when asked about the latter two requests. He also requested the farm animals not be delivered until he had trained his dogs.

After the initial shock, his parents concluded it just might be the very thing to redirect their directionless offspring. Following an intense family meeting, where the pros and cons of farming were discussed, the Marquis De Bluette arranged to have several acres in the north quadrant fenced off. In the centre, a small building was erected near a stream, along with a few pens for chickens and pigs. The cows and sheep had a large area inside the boundary.

People were forbidden to approach the place. Many a titter and guffaw was exchanged throughout the fiefs when, for the next few weeks, various horn cadences were heard emanating from the secluded farm. It was said, though never proven, that someone had sneaked up and then reported that the dogs moved in specific patterns in response to Robert's horn.

After a while it became routine and no one paid any attention.

A few months later, Robert asked to have his livestock delivered. He also mentioned that he would soon invite the le monde general (folks) to see his 'automated' farm in operation.

Once again the various horn toots rolled out over the hills and became part of the daily custom. It was noted however that the sounds seemed to have an altered intensity.

Then one day a strange eerie restlessness descended upon the countryside. At first the people could not pin-point the problem until they became aware that no sounds were echoing from the small isolated farm.

Finally, after many complaints about sheep being all over the fields and strange cows in the gardens, the Marquis rode out to investigate. As he approached his son's farm he saw chickens running around among broken fences and pigs rooting in the potato patch.

There was no sign of Robert. The Marquis became very concerned.

In desperation he called out in a loud booming voice, "Little Boy Bluette, come blow your horn. The sheep's in the meadow and the cow is in the corn!"

Although he vanished many years ago, Robert De Bluette has forever been remembered in song and verse.

The Elephant that Wanted to Join the Circus

Once upon a time there was an elephant that really liked peanuts, but there were no peanuts where he lived. He was not happy.

He wanted to join the circus because he heard people threw peanuts at elephants. Everybody liked elephants. Maybe he could even help out a little bit.

So, he started off to find a circus. On the way he met a bear.

"Hi, Bear. I'm off to join the circus."

"Not a good idea," said Bear. "I know. I was in the circus once."

"Really! What did you do?"

"I had to stand on my back legs and hold a ball."

"I can hold a ball with my trunk. Holding a ball is easy. They will give me peanuts."

"I had to wear a thing around my mouth," added Bear.

"Well they can't put one on me because my tusks will get in the way. Besides, I have to eat my peanuts."

"And I was kept in a cage."

The elephant thought about this.

"They don't make cages big enough for me," he said. "Well, I have to go now."

Off went the elephant. He walked and walked until he met a lion.

"Hi, Lion. I'm going to join the circus, so that I can have lots of peanuts."

"Not a good idea," said Lion. "I was in the circus once."

"Really? What did you do?"

"I had to jump through a fire hoop."

"I won't have to do that. I can't jump," said Elephant. "I'm going to hold a ball, and they will give me peanuts."

"They kept me in a cage."

"They don't make cages my size," said Elephant. "Well, goodbye, Lion. I have to go now."

Off went the elephant. He walked and walked until he met a monkey rubbing his neck.

"Hi, Monkey. I'm going to join the circus."

"Not a good idea," said Monkey.

"What's wrong with your neck?" asked Elephant.

"I just ran away from the circus. I had to wear a collar and a silly hat all the time."

"I am going to hold a ball so they will give me lots of peanuts."

"I would rather have no collar and no peanuts."

"They won't make a collar for me. My neck is too big."

"Maybe not, but they will put one around your leg and chain it to a post."

Elephant thought about this.

"I thought they needed a cage."

"Not for elephants," said Monkey. "They just use a leg collar."

"But, they will give me lots of peanuts."

"Not really. The elephants got hay and water."

"No peanuts?"

"I got more peanuts than the elephants," said Monkey.

"But, I'm bigger."

"It doesn't matter: Monkeys are cuter."

Elephant thought about this.

"I don't think I want to join the circus any more," said Elephant. "I think I'll go home."

"Good idea, Elephant," said Monkey. "Bye."

"Bye," said Elephant, and he went home and ate leaves, and lived happily ever after.

The Frog Prince

Alas! I am doomed to spend my life by this pond near
the King's well. Oh, woe is me! To be reduced to a common
amphibian, relegated to eating flies and grubs while constantly
on guard for herons, snakes, and most of all, that brat princess
yelling, "Kiss the frog, Kiss the frog", while trying to catch me.
If she weren't so damn spoiled she wouldn't be half bad.

You'd think she was hiding some weird secret.

But for now I shall exist – I shall persevere – for the day I
can slowly snuff the life out of that witch who changed me into
a frog.

I shall never forget the acrid smell of that puff of smoke.

I would have thought my father, the king, would have missed
me a lot more. But, oh no, he certainly wasted no time installing
my brother as next in line for the throne.

Oh well. Meanwhile, I'll hop over to the wishing well where
there are usually some flies hovering around the food scraps
dropped by the people who throw coins. A full tummy never
hurt anyone.

Drat, here comes that miserable kid bouncing her favourite
ball. If she sees me, she'll hammer me with it. Heaven knows
what would happen if she ever lost the thing.

Oops, now she's done it. She wasn't watching out for the

wishing well. She won't get it out without some help. Now maybe there will be some peace around here.

Aw, man! What an irritating whining howl! She's crying over that stupid ball. I'll let her howl; serves her right for chasing me all the time. I'll just ignore her.

She's getting louder!

I can't stand it!

I really don't know if I should take the chance, but it is the only way to stop that howling. It may also be the best opportunity I have to break this spell.

Oh well, better dead than green. I'll jump up on the rim.

'Er, hi Princess.' – I wish I could smile – 'No! No! Please don't be alarmed. Yes, it's me talking; the frog you always chase. I am actually a prince. A wicked witch changed into a frog.'

'You understand? Really? That's wonderful!'

How come she understands?

'Why are you crying?'

'I see. It's a good thing it's hollow. What will you give me if I retrieve your ball for you?'

I just love that look on her face.

'A surprise? Something very special? Okay, I'll trust you.'

Well, here goes nothing. Something tells me I'm making a terrible mistake, but I'm committed. A prince never goes back on his word.

There, that wasn't too difficult.

'Here's your ball. Now what is my surprise?'

Oh, no! Ooph! She grabbed me – well, it's not too tight. Oh no! She's going to eat me! – aw, yuk! I've been kissed!'

That is strange. I've smelled that smoke somewhere before.

And where did this beautiful femme fatale frog come from?

'Er, good morning, ma'am. Please pardon my impertinence, but you were not here a second ago. A wicked witch changed you into princess! That's terrific! I mean, how awful. Perhaps you will allow me offer you a little something back at my lily pad.'

Hmmm, maybe pond life won't be so bad after all.

The Gift

The chief engineer studied the sandstone mountain, and then turned to Jeremy.

"They want to put a forest lookout tower up there, so just cut a rough road around up to the top. You'll be on your own, and since you know how to operate all the equipment, you shouldn't have any problems. Radio if you need a hand drilling and blasting and I'll send up the crew."

Jeremy looked at the line of huge new machines.

"That big D-16 should be enough to do most of the work," continued the Forman. "That Michigan is almost brand new. Well, I gotta go."

Jeremy never had time to ask questions or say good-bye, but that was Harold.

The big CAT roared into action, and was soon chewing out the hillside. The dislodged material was pushed over the edge as the road took shape. Jeremy found it relatively easy.

About a third of the way up, he decided to cut out a large cavern which would allow vehicles to pass.

He called for the blasting crew, and enjoyed how they blew the material out and over the edge of the cliff.

When they were done, he drove the front-end loader up the hill to clean up their mess, and finish cleaning out the cave.

With that job completed, Jeremy continued cutting the road as wide as the D-16 blade, pushing the rock over the sides but careful not to go too far himself.

When he wanted to make another passing cave, he decided not to call the blasters, but do it himself with the Michigan. Jeremy enjoyed the front-end loader's roar – it was a change from the D-16 – as it scooped out the soft sand stone.

He looked at the road, and wondered how good it really was and if Harold would approve. He should drive the pickup up the mountain because it would be a good indicator as to where the road needed more work.

The half-ton grumbled along as it crawled up the newly-created road. Jeremy was quite pleased with his work.

"Not bad," he thought to himself. "Oops! There's a spot to fix." And he laughed.

Eventually, he drove the truck back down and resumed working with the D-16 to cut the last section of road. The engine noise was terrible but Jeremy was getting used to it.

He noticed he had almost gone completely around the hill. So now, as he ploughed, he had to be careful not to damage the lower sections. It was a bit awkward, but Jeremy enjoyed the challenge.

Finally, he was at the top and ahead of schedule too. The chief engineer would be very pleased – might even give him a raise. Right now, before the boss came back, he should use the little truck to test the completed road again.

He parked the CAT, started the half-ton, and smiled inwardly as he guided the truck to the top. He particularly liked the tread marks the tires left in the sand.

With the truck at the top, Jeremy stuffed his hands in his pockets and proudly stared out across the countryside. He felt pretty good almost as if he had carved out his own place in history.

"Myrtle," said Ethel, to her friend beside her on the park bench, "that Thompson boy has been playing on that huge sand pile all morning."

"So he has," came the predictable response. "Imagination is such a wonderful gift."

A Tough Customer

The cool weather made for a slow day at my thirty flavours ice cream parlour. I was bent over behind the sherbet case when I heard the entry bell clang, and an authoritative voice say, "Take your time, boy, lots to pick from here."

When I stood up, the man looked over at me and added, "Kid's not much for fries – wanted ice cream. I want a burger and fries from next door."

I nodded understandably and then smiled at what appeared to be about a five year old.

"Meet us over at the picnic tables when you're done son," said the dad, handing the child a few bills.

The bell clanged behind him.

"Come on in," I motioned and came around from behind the counter. I pointed to the four freezers.

"This cooler has the ones people pick the most. This one has some interesting variations, and this one," I pointed to the cooler marked EXOTIC, "has some really different ones."

The boy, who appeared to be small for his age, politely followed my gestures.

"And if you like Sherbets," (I could tell he did not), "there are some over there."

When he edged towards the first freezer, I saw that he was going to be too short to have a good look.

Grabbing the step stool I said, "Here stand on this."

After he was on, I went behind the counter.

"Would you like me to tell you the flavours?"

A tiny nod and large brown eyes told me 'yes', and an appreciative smile glimmered.

"Well, as I said before, since these are the ones most people choose, I put them all together. Starting in the front row, that one on your left, is Vanilla, then it's Chocolate, Strawberry, and Butterscotch"

I looked up. "That's my favourite."

The little guy showed no reaction, so I carried on.

"In the second row it's Banana, Double Chocolate Fudge and Orange. The four here in the back, are Maple Walnut...."

"Don't like walnuts," he interrupted.

"Well, okay, that's fine," I said, glad to have some sort of reaction. "Umm, then there is Mint Chocolate, Black Cherry and Butter Pecan."

"Don't like pecans, neither."

"Yeah," I agreed. "I'm not much for pecans myself."

'Hey,' I mused, 'The customer is always right, even if he is small.'

I waited while he surveyed the containers.

"Anything interest you?"

When there was no decision, I came around to the front.

"Maybe something in this next case will tempt your taste buds," I smiled, easing him off the stool and sliding it over to the next cooler.

The entry bell clanged. A 'Hi Ernie' greeted me from the door as Harold came barrelling in.

"Must be one o'clock," I answered. "The usual, with double chocolate on the bottom?"

"Yup. Just because it's cool today, doesn't mean I can't have my cone."

"Excuse me while I look after Harold," I motioned to the boy. "Meanwhile have a peek in there to see if there is something you might like."

As I scooped out a large ball of double chocolate fudge, I saw Harold looking at the child.

"Who's your big customer?"

"Don't know his name, but he doesn't like walnuts."

Harold bent down towards the boy. "I don't 'em either, kid," he bellowed. "You're not missing anything."

The boy turned and gave him a deadpan stare.

"I don't like pecans, neither."

"Hey, that's okay." Harold retreated from the look.

Meanwhile, as I completed his cone by putting a large scoop of chocolate on top, he gestured towards the child.

"Tough customer yuh have there, Ern," he laughed. "See you tomorrow."

After he left, I looked over the freezer. The head didn't move while the eyes surveyed the containers.

"Would you like to know what these are? They are a little more specialized."

There was a small nod.

"Well, down there in the front row, it is French Vanilla, Coconut Cream, Peppermint Stick, and Banana Split."

There wasn't a flicker, so I continued.

"The middle three are Blueberry Vanilla, Cherry Cheese Cake, and Chocolate Raspberry Truffle."

I had a feeling these weren't his style.

"And across the back," I added some flair, "are Cookies and Cream, Cinnamon Swirl, Pistachio and Chocolate Almond."

"Don't like almonds."

"That's fine."

As I waited, a couple came in. I excused myself.

After serving one each a double of Strawberry and Butter Scotch, I returned to my small customer. The child hadn't moved.

"Perhaps you would like something more exotic," I suggested. From the look, I knew it was the wrong word.

"What I mean is: do you feel like trying something really different?"

Receiving the usual non-reaction, I went around to the front and moved the stool to the front of the third case.

The boy looked at the wild colours with the same disdain.

I was glad it was a slow day.

"Finally, for your enjoyment," I felt like a circus announcer, "are the real fancy flavours. Starting at the front at your left are Bubblegum, Liquorice, M and M's, and Hawaiian Cherry Garden. The three in the middle are Smurf, Rocky Road and Peanut Butter."

I stopped.

"Oops! Sorry. You probably don't like peanuts."

The deep brown eyes looked up.

"I like peanuts."

"Oh, that's great. Finally, in the last row, we have Moose Tracks, Mud Pie, Tin Roof and Kitchen Sink."

I could tell these were not making much of an impression.

I wondered if there was a choice in the offering.

"Well, what will it be?" I urged trying to initiate some sort of decision.

Suddenly, he stepped off the stool, decisively kicked it over to the first case, climbed up and pointing said, "I'll want two big scoops of that."

"Vanilla! After all that, you want vanilla?

The beaming smile showed it had been worth the effort.

He offered his money when I handed him the extra large cone.

I closed his hand over the bills. "It's on the house. You made my day."

The bell clanged as I let him out and waved after him.

"Goodbye. Thanks for coming."

I watched until he arrived at his parents' lunch table.

Although I knew he was out of earshot, I said softly, "Come back again."

The clang of the bell seemed louder than usual as it reverberated in my now-empty ice cream parlour. Somehow the rest of the day was going to be anticlimactic.

Metamorphosis

I came to a puffing gritty halt. My proposed stroll had turned into vicious undirected march.

In an attempt to escape my life's perceived pointlessness, I had told my wife I was going for a walk, and in answer to her 'Where?' I snapped, "I dunno – just out."

Once on the park trail, the suppressed anger at my seemingly meaningless existence had insidiously transferred itself into my pace and had transformed it to an intense stride.

I was going nowhere very fast.

Offset in a grove of bushes an isolated bench beckoned. I plopped onto it as a wave of panic washed over me. I buried my face in my hands.

After fifty plus years, I had not accomplished a thing of worldly significance. Who was this Henry Walker anyway? If I died, the plant would have another supervisor before the doctor closed the file. It was great to see Maryanne become head of the I.C.U. where they needed her. As for the kids: both were doing well after I helped them through university. They certainly didn't need me now.

Resting my chin in my hands, I scowled at some ants in their usual frenetic pursuit of tidbits. A cricket invaded my peripheral vision as it scuttled under the leaves. I glanced at the spider waiting in the middle of her web spun beneath the bench, and I wondered if she was as bored as I was.

It was then I noticed a splash of orange in the grass. Retrieving the entity, my heart softened as the huge Monarch Butterfly lay brittle and stiff on my hand.

'What a pathetic life! What a waste of time,' I groused as my mind sequenced through the insect's life stages. 'What irrelevancy: to hatch, then do nothing more than to eat and eat and eat until inside the chrysalis metamorphosis transforms the bloated caterpillar into a thing of frail beauty whose existence radiates upon the world for a short but spectacular time.'

I resented the creature. At least it was noticed and admired. I was like one of those scouring ants scrambling around inside an indifferent society; a culture that does not know I exist – or even care.

I was just 'an ant'.

I glanced at other folks out enjoying the sunshine. I inwardly sniggered figuring that quite probably they were 'ants' also.

"Not too many 'butterflies' there," I mused aloud.

Suddenly I realized that at any one point in human history, there were very few 'butterflies'. Some people blossomed briefly but were soon forgotten. Only a tiny number achieve anything spectacular and impressive.

Was it not therefore of higher importance to excel in one's own environment – to inspire the values one holds dear and precious upon the next generation – to be remembered, hopefully, as 'a star' in one's own sphere of influence? Could it not be argued: The Almighty smiles upon those who aspire to do their best?

An African Proverb came to mind: A man is not dead until he is forgotten.

Internal reconciliation dissolved the mists of doubt gripping my mind and heart.

I stood up and relished the warmth emanating from the early evening sun on its slow decent upon the horizon.

I think I'll take Mary out to her favourite restaurant, and try to explain the reason for my testiness.

She probably already knows anyway.

Miss-Placed

Oberon reined in his horse, reached back, and swung Eveleth around and down to the ground where she stumbled backward into a rather undignified pile.

Scrambling to her feet she yelled, "You can't leave me out here!"

Oberon scratched an imaginary itch. "I have to. The contract was for the prettiest girl. The Queen said I was to take the prettiest girl out into the forest and leave her there, and that's what I did."

"You came to the wrong house!"

"Oh no, you're not gonna fool me. I went to the castle and there was no one there except a dirty girl in rags."

"She was the one! Snow White!!"

"Well she didn't look too pretty to me."

"She's the one you were supposed to take! Not me!"

"Well, you're the prettiest in the town alright, and the Queen said to take the prettiest girl and I always liked the way you just sat around, and did nothing so you could stay nice and clean."

"That's because Cinderella did all the housework!"

"I don't know nothin' about no Cinderella. All I know is I have been kind of a watchin' you 'n' stuff."

"Oh, you are so stupid! You have me mixed up with Snow White, the Queen's step daughter!"

Oberon scratched his head.

"And you can't just dump me off in the middle of nowhere!"

"I have to on a count of the Queen said I had to, so I gone and done it."

"But, the Queen doesn't run our house!

"Now, you just let go my horse, 'cause I hafta get back or the Queen'll wonder what's goin' on, and I don't feel like tryin' to 'splain things. I brang you here 'cause I happen to know there's a large shack over there that you can stay in."

"A shack!"

"Uh-huh. Not too far – over that way – a real nice one."

"I can't live in a shack!"

"Well, you're gonna have to, leastwise until the Queen says you can come back."

"But the Queen is not mad at me, you big dummy!"

"Maybe so, and maybe not, but now you jus' go along there, and find that shack."

"You can't do this to me!"

"Yes, I can, on a count of the Queen said so and I have to do what the Queen says, or she'll get mad at me, and then I'll have to take myself out into the woods and leave me there—- Huh! Huh! That's a pretty good joke, doncha think?"

"You'd get lost in your own shirt, you nit".

"Well maybe when she quits being mad at you, I can come back and get you."

"You have it all wrong, you big stupid clod! You've grabbed the wrong person!"

"You can call me all the names you want to, but I knows what I have to do. I also brang you this here bag of things you might need."

"Things? What 'things'?"

"Oh, scrub brushes and cleaning rags.

"What!"

"And lots of soap."

"What!".

"You'll probably have to keep house for the seven little miners that live there."

"I don't know anything about housekeeping!"

"Well, you're gonna have to learn pretty quick, 'cause I gotta get back before the queen begins wondering what happened. Now, you take care."

With a twinge of panic setting in, she watched woodsman disappear. "But, you have it all wrong," Eveleth mumbled after him.

'This can't be happening'. She grabbed the bag and headed in the direction the big dope had pointed. She'd get even with Cinderella and Snow White later, but right now, with evening approaching, she'd better find that shack.

She smiled evilly; thinking how the fur will fly when the Queen discovers the woodsman had taken the wrong girl.

He'd be back tomorrow to get her; she just had to survive the night.

After stumbling along for a while, Eveleth thought she saw something silhouetted in a clump of trees. She blinked and looked again. It was the shack – no – a large log house almost hidden by the forest.

She ran and knocked on the door. When there was no answer to her third rap, she peered through a dirty window. It crossed her mind that no one could possibly live here, because the place was such a mess. Should she go in, just to get out of the weather? Maybe she should wait.

A flash of lightning followed by an almost simultaneous crash of thunder, decided the situation. She hurried inside, slammed the door and leaned against it.

The overwhelming stench of dirty dishes, unwashed clothes and garbage nearly drove her outside again.

At that very moment, her heart froze when she heard the distant voices of a male choir singing, Hi-Ho. Hi-Ho. It's home from work we go....

Another Time – Same place

The author relaxed at the keyboard and then opened a long-neglected, unfinished story.

Hi.

Hi.

I'm glad you're back.

Yes, finally.

I've missed you.

I missed you too.

It's been a long time.

Too long.

Where did you go?

I've been busy.

Oh sure; probably with other characters.

There were priorities; deadlines, contests, the like.

You know I can't live without you!

Yes but...

Even time has no meaning.

I understand that but...

I come alive when you are around.

I know, but so do many others.

You introduced me to that mysterious gentleman who was, shall we say, interested.

I remember.

And that intimate dining experience was extraordinary.

The Moroccan Kasbah Restaurant; I thought you'd like that.

I'm still wearing that low-cut black gown and the pearls.

Good.

My hair is perfect.

You look great.

And Henry was saying all the right things and giving signals.

Anticipation is half the fun.

Yes! But just as things were warming up, you left!

I had a contest deadline.

What about MY deadline? I'm looking forward to getting – well – you know....

Exactly; well, let's see what I can do.

The author began writing.

Full Circle

I'm here! I'm really here! I wish Dad were alive – he would be so proud.

It seems quiet now that the engine has stopped – just the clicking of the switches and the metallic ticking of the Lunar Module rapidly cooling.

Strange how I never noticed the hum of the air re-circulation system before this, but the tiny air currents certainly makes one appreciate one of life's basic necessities, especially in a place like this.

Well, might as well get on with it. I was not sent all this way to sit around.

"Roger, Houston, EVA in five. Here, Henry, let me check you out, then you can do me."

I really don't care if I'm not the first one here, but I am the first in this particular sector because they want us to check out that interesting rocky ridge.

I cannot get over the utter silence; even my breathing seems loud. The awareness of feeling my footsteps rather than hearing them is a bit peculiar. The radio static is irritating – seems to spoil the mood somehow.

Everything is some shade of grey except where the sun,

which is amazingly bright, creates vivid contrasting black shadows. In this reduced gravity it is remarkable how much further the dust travels.

Oh God, what a sight! The earth is a huge blue ball suspended against an ebony star studded – what were Dr. Sagan's words: billions and billions? – background. It is the exact converse to that big ol' harvest moon Dad and I watched many years ago.

It was only yesterday, when after a day of chores, we were relaxing on the porch swing – Dad with his Budweiser and I with my Coke – and were reviewing the day's events and enjoying the sights, sounds and smells of the farm at night; the wind rattling the dried corn stalks, Mom's television programme coming from the living room, the periodic whine of an irritating mosquito, the ever-present pervasive aroma of 'cow', and the occasional squeak from the swing's hinges.

Then, just as we were about to go inside, that big ol' golden harvest moon peaked over that corn patch. Immersed in our thoughts, we watched it's slow inevitable ascent until it was fully perched above the tassels.

"You know, Dad," I stated, "Someday I'm going to walk on that moon."

"I'm sure you will, son," he'd smiled. "Just study hard and keep that goal in mind."

I wish he could see me now.

Maybe he can.

A Night
on the Town

"Hey, Spike, what makes you so certain she'll be here tonight?" I asked for the third time in as many minutes.

My hesitant question became somewhat lost as an autumn gust swirled through the darkened alley.

I was huddled behind Mix's emaciated body, which in turn was scrunched at the back of Spike's massiveness. Under his heavy coat, it was difficult to tell where Spike's head ended and his shoulders began. In contrast, Mix's sharp angular features seemed to beg for further insulation.

"For the last time," Spike snarled, "I heard it from Trixy, see, and Trixy don't tell me no lies; so, just be quiet, understand?"

"Yeah," echoed Mix. "Understand?"

I persevered. "Well, what if she doesn't show?"

"She'll show."

"Yeah, she'll show," Mix repeated.

"Maybe you have the dates mixed up," I tentatively suggested.

Spike glared back.

"I don't makes no mistakes."

"Yeah, Spike don't make no mistakes."

I glared at the scrawny face. "Mix," I spat, "have you ever considered creating your own conversations?"

He looked to Spike for support, but he only received a shrug, and found himself looking at Spike's back again.

The skinny punk ticked me off.

"Mix," I persisted, "if I want something from you, I'll address you personally. Do you understand?"

"I was just trying to..."

"I don't care what you were trying to do. Just...just...quit being such a parrot."

"Both of you shut up."

"Yea..."

Mix's response froze in his throat as Spike's scarred nose was suddenly an inch from his, and pushing him up against the wall.

"Look, if I need a seconder, I'll ask for one."

"Sure, Spike, I was just agreeing with you."

"Do I need you to okay my decisions?"

"Gosh, no, Spike."

Mix shot me a malicious look as he could see I was enjoying the exchange.

"Do I ever ask you for your opinion?"

"Um, well, no."

"Then get off Curly's back!"

"I was just trying to help."

"Stop trying to help," Spike snapped, then sneered, "You wanna help?"

Mix nodded vigorously.

"Don't help!"

Slowly and deliberately, Spike turned to face the alley's

opening, just as another cold blast stirred up the dust and rearranged the papers.

Mix leaned closer to me.

"Spike's a little touchy tonight."

"I wouldn't know. It's my first time here."

"Yeah," queried Mix, "how come Spike asked you to come along anyway?"

"Well, the other day when Spike passed by my door, I mentioned how his life seemed to be more exciting than mine. So he invited me to join him tonight."

"How did you get out?"

"I just asked."

"Gosh, I'd never do that, 'specially if I had good clothes like you."

I glanced at Mix's ratty coat and dirty hands. "Aren't you going home later?"

"Don't have no home."

"Oh, I'm sorry."

"I ran away, and when I did go back, my family had moved."

"That's awful!"

"I've been with Spike ever since. He's been a sorta dad for me."

Spike swung around. "What are you two blithering about back here?"

"Er, nothing, Spike," I stammered.

"Yeah, nothing, Spike." Mix flashed me a tiny grin.

"If you guys spoil tonight for me, the fur's gonna fly."

The light from an overhead window illuminated Spike's chiselled features, but before he could snap into the shadows, I saw tired furtive eyes peering from a defensive battle-scarred face.

When the light went off the alley seemed darker and dirtier.

"Spike," I began gently, "how long have you been knocking around in places like this?"

"Long time…years…ever since I was thrown out."

"Oh, I am sorry."

"It wasn't my fault."

"Of course not." I could tell it was a touchy subject.

"Well, it wasn't."

"I'm not arguing, Spike."

"I've done all right for myself."

"Of course you have," I granted, but my eyes betrayed me when they strayed to the boxes and bins.

"Yeah," Mix defended. "Spike's done all right for himself."

"Nobody pushes me around."

"Yeah, nobody pushes Spike around," chipped Mix.

Spike turned ever-so-slowly towards Mix, and in a voice that sounded very old and extremely tired said, "Mix, for once in your life, please be quiet."

Spike's giant face softened when he faced me.

"Look kid, I know you were looking for some excitement tonight, but it just aint gonna happen."

"But," I began, "I thought we…"

"Yeah, yeah, I know, but it was a stupid idea."

"Yeah, a stupid idea."

"MIX!" yelled Spike, "One of these days…"

"Sorry, Spike." Mix shrunk back into the shadows.

Spike returned to me.

"This here place aint no place for the likes of you. It's best you go back home; at least you have one."

"Yeah, a home," came a sad echo.

The longing in their voices was unmistakeable.

"You're sure?" I asked.

"Yeah, I'm sure."

"Yeah, me too," agreed Mix."

"Well, okay," I sighed, "if you think so."

"Yeah, I think that would be best solution."

"Yeah, the best," came the 'echo'.

"G'bye, kid," Spike smiled sadly. "See you around."

"Yeah," chimed Mix, "see you around, Curly."

Thus, with mixed feelings, I bade the two of them good-bye. Then ensuring my tail had its proper curl, I scampered home where a saucer of milk and a bowl of Meow-Mix was waiting.

Old Bart's Legacy

Jeremy did not understand funerals and he certainly did not want to understand this one.

Old Bart was dead. The old artist — the only one who had ever treated him like a real person — was about to disappear forever.

The cold damp morning added to his misery as he stood beside his mother in the cemetery. He felt all mixed up as he remembered his wonderful friend.

Some kids had called Old Bart "The Monster" due to the scars all over his face and hands. People didn't know — or had forgotten — how Bart had tried to save his family from the fire. Jeremy often listened to Old Bart while, with tears running down his cracked cheeks and hands clawing the air, he told and retold that terrible memory.

But it was those hands with their bent fingers that Jeremy liked best. He could not understand how fingers so stiff and twisted could create such beautiful paintings — pictures that were almost alive.

His eyes blurred as he remembered finding his old friend lying beside his easel at their favourite painting spot. When he knew there was nothing he could do, Jeremy sat beside him, gently held a gnarled hand, and cried for a long time.

It was there at the lake, as another piece of the world was being captured on canvas that the artist answered Jeremy's many questions about life, attitudes, and school — almost everything his mom wouldn't talk about.

One day when Jeremy got brave enough to ask why mean kids teased him and sometimes called him "Stupid" or "Dummy" or even "Downsie ", Old Bart sighed and explained how Mother Nature doesn't make everyone the same. Jeremy was one of those special people. He looked into Jeremy's eyes and smiled, "It is the human adventure to discover the talent lying hidden within each of us." It helped a little bit, because it was usually at night he remembered those words, and repeated them over and over before falling asleep.

Although Jeremy was old enough to be on his own, he lived with his mom, but spent most of the time at Old Bart's place.

His lips tightened. He remembered the first time he had used some paints and when he had proudly shown his picture to his mom she'd laughed. After that he kept his paintings under Old Bart's counter.

He never told his mom how much he liked painting birds and animals, or how much he was learning. Jeremy figured he must have been improving because his friend began spending more time showing colour mixing and teaching him other strokes.

One day Old Bart said, "I like the way you paint, Jeremy. There is a basic honesty in your work, a mystical inward sincerity. You certainly have a unique style. There is really not much more I can teach you."

Jeremy wasn't quite sure what all that meant, but he figured if Old Bart said it, it must be all right.

Jeremy peered at the faces of the people standing around the coffin and wondered if they had come to say good-bye or just wanted to visit.

His mom yanked his arm. "Stop staring," she ordered.

"I wasn't," he protested a little too loudly. "I was just looking."

"Well, don't look like that."

"How am I supposed to see if I don't look?"

"I'll explain later." Her face stiffened.

She never did explain things later.

"And please keep your mouth closed," she hissed in his ear. "It's so embarrassing."

Jeremy chewed on his lip. His teachers were the same. They never explained anything either, and always told him that things were too hard for him. He knew he was not smart at school stuff. It was hard to understand how the same numbers could give different answers. Reading was tough too, because the letters kept changing shape. But once the morning math and reading lessons were over, he was allowed to draw, paint and colour as much as he wanted, just keep out of the teacher's way.

It went on for years.

But Jeremy could read. He could read people.

He glanced sideways at crinkly Old Miss Tweed hiding under her black netting. He never liked her — her and her dried-apple face. She had a sort of crusty look, but she never died! She always went to other people's funerals.

Right now, there was something unfair about that.

Every so often Miss Tweed came to the studio. She would peer over her nose-glasses and say, "Yes, I see," as the artist told her about the paintings. Jeremy knew she didn't. Eventually, she would choose some and Old Bart would put them in her car.

He noticed how his friend never showed Miss Tweed the ones he kept in the large locked cupboard. Every once in a while, Bart would carefully pack these into large padded containers, and send them to a place called a gallery. Lately, Old Bart had been including some of Jeremy's pictures. The gallery people must have liked them because the paintings never came back.

Jeremy remembered asking Old Bart why he did not charge her very much. "She's got lots of money, you know."

"I don't need her money," he'd answered. "She bought what she wanted. I ask enough so that she thinks she is keeping me in paints, brushes and canvases."

Then he stroked his patchy grey whiskers and said, "It gives some purpose to her life. She may be rich and have a fancy house, but way down deep inside, she is hurting. A long time ago, someone or something must have happened to make her shut people out. I just do my best to encourage her."

After a long pause he added, "You know, Jeremy, a person should strive to do as much good as possible in his lifetime."

Jeremy's eyes flew open. He thought of the big white letter!

One day, Old Bart had asked him to come into the cabin. Jeremy knew something was different because his friend was very serious.

"Please sit down, Jeremy. I need to talk to you."

Jeremy happily plunked himself into his favourite kitchen chair.

From a drawer, the Old Bart removed a big white letter and

placed it on the table. Although it was a fancy envelope, Jeremy knew L.L.D. wasn't a real word.

Old Bart took a deep breath.

"This," he said, tapping the white packet, "is a very important document. It tells a lawyer to leave all this," — his hands moved slowly around the room — "to you when I'm gone."

Jeremy panicked. "Are you leaving?"

"No! No!" came a laugh. "It's not that kind of leaving."

Jeremy relaxed; maybe Bart was going to visit someone.

Bart took another deep breath.

"You must know that nobody lives forever. Some day, like everyone else, I'm going to die."

"When?"

Old Bart chuckled. "Well, not for a while yet I hope, but a person should plan ahead."

"Are you planning to die?"

Bart man snapped. No, I'm not planning to die." He reached across the table and patted Jeremy's hand. "My young friend, before they die, most people want to do something for their friends and family."

Jeremy nodded, trying to understand the conversation.

Old Bart's lips cracked a smile. "You have been coming to visit me for years, and we have shared many good times. Meanwhile, you have become quite a good artist."

"You mean I'm an artist?"

"Yes, but right now, let me finish."

Jeremy leaned forward and squinted to listen better.

"You have become more than an artist. I lost my family

many years ago, and since then you have become the closest thing to a family I have had."

Bart paused and then went on, "When I die, I have arranged for this cabin, the land and my paintings to become yours."

Again Old Bart let the words sink in, and then added, "You will own everything."

Jeremy felt as if Old Bart was staring right through him.

"Do you understand what I'm telling you?"

"I think so," Jeremy nodded slowly, but was starting to feel cold and very uncomfortable.

Old Bart continued. "Now, I have seen to all the technicalities. A man called a trustee will see that my wishes are carried out." The artist leaned forward. "Do you understand all this?"

Jeremy stopped nodding and, scrunched in the chair, and looked at his hands in his lap. He did not like what Old Bart was telling him.

"I have also set up a trust fund through the gallery, which will be promoting your work."

"Was that what all those papers were for?" Jeremy mumbled, remembering the day a man with a small suitcase had come to see Old Bart. After talking together for a long time, they asked Jeremy to come into the kitchen and put his name beside Bart's name.

"Yes, that was all part of it."

Old Bart straightened up. "Now, Jeremy, please tell me what I have just told you."

Jeremy shook his head and stared at his hands.

"Come on," Old Bart urged gently.

Jeremy shook his head harder.

"I know it's difficult."

Jeremy buried his face in his hands.

"Please try," urged Old Bart. "I need to know that you understand the situation."

With tears running down his face, and with a few tender prompts from Old Bart, Jeremy haltingly recited his understanding of what he had just been told. Suddenly, he yelled, "But I don't want you to die!"

Old Bart chuckled. "Well, I plan to be around for some time yet."

Jeremy smiled weakly, snuffling into his sleeve while wiping his eyes. He did not like the word "yet".

Old Bart stood up. "Come on, Jeremy, we're burning daylight."

Jeremy reluctantly followed Old Bart to their spot, but painting did not go well that afternoon.

Jeremy tugged on his mom's sleeve.

"Mom! Mom! There's a letter! A big white letter!"

She scowled at him.

"Not now, Jeremy." She turned back to the minister's droning.

"Bart had big important letter made for me."

"Not...now...Jeremy," she spat, her teeth clenched.

Jeremy knew he would have to wait until the minister was finished. It seemed to take forever. Finally, the people relaxed and talked normally. Moments later, a well-dressed man appeared beside his mother.

It was the suitcase man!

"Mrs. Wellesley?" he asked.

"Yes," said his mom, somewhat guardedly.

"Allow me to introduce myself," he said, handing her a card. "I am Brian Stevens from the Law Office of Stevens, Stevens, and Brock. I'd like to arrange an appointment with you, at your earliest convenience, regarding the estate of the late Mr. Bartholomew Lawrence."

He turned and smiled directly at Jeremy.

"It concerns Jeremy."

Jeremy smiled back.

Why Pigs
Have Curly Tails

Once upon a time, pigs had lovely long straight tails. They were very proud of their tails because they had many uses. The pigs could signal one another; tails could point in different directions; tails could swat flies; and tails could scratch some places.

The pigs knew their tails should never get soaking wet. A bit of rain wouldn't hurt them, but they could not go swimming.

If the pigs became a little bit dirty, they would find some fresh thick grass in the morning and scrub around in it. But, if they became really dirty, then they would carefully slip into a quiet pool and let the dirt sort of soak off. They would keep their tails straight up out of the water.

Well, one day, when the pigs were play wrestling, they did not notice they were in a blue berry patch. They pulled and pushed, scratched and squealed until they were all tired out.

When they stopped to rest, they looked at each other.

What a mess!

EVERYONE HAD BIG BLUE AND PURPLE STAINS!

They ran to their favourite long grass area, where they rolled around, rubbing and scrubbing.

Some stains came off.

Most didn't.

They knew they would have to take a bath!

They could tell by the trees that the wind was blowing just a little bit. They would have to take the chance. At the lake, they slowly crept into the water, and hoped the cool water would wash off the rest of the stains.

It seemed to be working!

Just as they decided to come out, a huge moose burst out of the bush and splashed into the pond. A huge wave washed over the pigs.

"Oh, no!" they yelled.

The pigs ran up the hill and sat in the sun. They held their tails very stiff and straight. It was hard to keep their tails that way for a long time. But, as the sun dried the top of the tail, the bottom part was still damp. The dry part shrank, like wool does, and the tails started to curl!

There was nothing they could do!

Oh, how the pigs cried!

So, that is why pigs have curly tails today!

Ship Repairs

It was such a lovely Saturday morning I had extended my customary walks a few extra blocks from the Senior Centre, while my trusty cane provided its usual entertainment as I poked at various pieces of trash along the sidewalk.

Not really paying attention to where I was going, I was somewhat startled when a pair of legs came into view. When I looked up, I saw a young lad of about eight or nine peering through the iron grating of a small side entrance to a cemetery.

I went closer and followed his gaze.

"Squirrel?"

After a quick glance at me, he shook his head, and mumbled, "My grandpa's in there."

"Oh, I'm sorry." I didn't know what else to say.

"He died last week. I sure miss him."

"I'll bet you do."

"They put him in *there*."

"Well, it looks nice and peaceful."

"He won't be happy."

"Why not?"

"He liked the bush. They should have buried him in the bush!"

Emphatic disappointment was unmistakable.

"Um, I don't think it's allowed any more."

"They could have found a way," he stated.

We stood there, staring at the setting – at the headstones – at nothing.

"Well, I gotta go," he said, and began moving off in the direction I had been walking.

"Mind if I walk with you, although I'm not quite as fast as you?"

"Sure."

"Tell me about your Grandpa. What was he like?"

His little face brightened.

"Oh, Grandpa was funny. We did things."

"What kind of things?"

"Sometimes we built kites. He never wanted to buy one. He always said, 'When I was your age, you built your own.'"

The kid smiled weakly at this recollection.

"Of course," I said, recalling my own kite building days. "Were they four-cornered or six-cornered?"

"What do you mean?"

I used my cane to draw in the dirt. "Well, did your kite look like this, or like this?"

"Oh, we made this kind, just two sticks. We used a garbage bag and tape to cover it. What kind did you make?"

"I made the extended hexagon type, and used tissue paper and glue. The tail was a long line of rags."

"No plastic?"

"There was no plastic in those days."

"Gosh, that must have been a long time ago."

"Yes," I chuckled. "I suppose it was."

"Grandpa had a cabin way up north, and last summer mom and dad let me go and stay with him for a whole month. We canoed and fished and did camping stuff."

"Sounds like it was a lot fun," I said, as we came upon a park bench and sat down.

"Yeah, it was really neat." The boy's eyes sparkled with obvious vivid memories. "Have you ever made a sailboat out of an old log?"

"Never," I said. "How do you do it?"

"Well," he began instructionally, "First you have to find a tree that has been dead for just the right amount of time. If it's too old, it will just fall apart."

"Sounds quite technical."

"Yeah, but if you find the perfect tree, you can make lots of boats out of it."

"So you just don't grab any log."

"Oh, no. It has to be hard on the outside and sort of soft in the middle. Then all you do is sharpen one end to make the front part – Grandpa did that – and then you find a thin stick for a mast, and make the point kind of flat so you can jamb it into the log."

"What did you use for sails?"

"Birch bark. You also hafta find a dead birch tree too. You're not supposed to take bark off a live one 'cause then it will die, at least that's what grandpa said."

"He was right."

"So then you just cut the bark the size you want, cut two holes and slide it down the stick."

"And away you go," I anticipated.

"Oh no," he said, looking straight at me. "You hafta put some lids on. At first, Grandpa did that, because he was afraid I might cut myself. He let me do it later on. Anyway, you stick one in the back, and pushed two into the bottom. The first boat we made went in a circle and came back."

"Well, that was pretty good."

The boy frowned a little. "Not really, 'cause it was supposed to keep going as if on a voyage. Grandpa bent the lids a little bit and then it went straight out across the lake."

"It certainly sounds like a lot of fun."

As he jabbered away, I began to think of playing simple computer games with my own Grandson, Daniel, whom I had not seen for quite awhile, all due to a silly misunderstanding. I should not have argued with Maryanne.

My stubborn pride had blocked reconciliation.

"Do you have grand kids?"

The question snapped me back to reality.

"Er, yes," I smiled, picturing Daniel's face, "One, a boy about your age."

"Do you do stuff together?"

"We used to. We haven't for some time now."

"How come?"

"Oh, I had an argument with my daughter – his mom. We got mad and said some things we shouldn't have. Actually, I said some things I shouldn't have. I can't even remember what the fight was about."

I laughed self-consciously. "I don't why I'm telling you all this."

"Did you fight with your grandson?"

"No."

"Don't you miss him?"

"Of course," I nodded.

"I'll bet he misses you."

Immediate realization set in. The priorities of life were far more important than maintaining some semblance of childish pride.

I stood up and shook his hand.

"Thank you, young man," I said, "for opening an old man's eyes. I shall go and rectify a situation which should have been resolved weeks ago."

I hurried home where, with some trepidation, I lifted the receiver and dialled.

Upon hearing the familiar voice at the other end, I said, "Er, hi, Maryanne. Um, I was wondering, if we could meet for a coffee and donut this afternoon."

The Day Dad Shot
My Fish

Dad's patience was legendary. His friends, workmates, and curling associates referred to this attribute in almost reverential tones. Quite likely, he could have given the prophet Job a few pointers.

But, the one time, the only time, I saw Dad really lose his temper was during a camping trip.

I'll elaborate.

Dad had planned a little three-day outing up the Grassy River into Tramping Lake where the pickerel fishing was usually quite exciting. Rather than have our own canoe, engine and gas trucked twenty miles down to the river, he had arranged to borrow a boat and motor from a friend who lived there.

Fine.

Everything went perfectly until we were on the river for about five minutes, when the little three-horse engine stopped. Dad pulled and pulled. Nothing. He adjusted the needle valve. The engine spluttered, and quit. Dad tried again. It coughed and died. I could see he was getting tired, along with a slow 'burn' beneath his controlled exterior. He adjusted the gas-flow valve. The engine roared, then quit. The tool kit came out with the tight words, "It must be dirty gas."

I was bored, as there was not much to do while floating

down the small meandering Grassy. I thought, 'Hey! It should be good fishing here, and our drifting is perfect for trolling.'

I looked at Dad, but I could tell it was not a good time to ask a question like "Would you mind if I fished while you're doing that?"

I clipped on a red-and-white Dare Devil and cast out.

A huge Northern Pike swirled under my hook just as it cleared the surface.

Wow! Now, if I could just catch that one!

I recast in the direction the big fish had gone. A massive pull showed it was well hooked.

At that same instant, the engine roared with strong renewed life. I could tell by the sound that it had been fixed. The forward motion of the boat, coupled with the pull of the great fish, threatened to break the heavy-duty nylon braided line.

In somewhat of a panic, I yelled, "Shut it off!"

"What?" he called back over the engine noise.

"Shut the engine off!" I yelled.

"WHAT!" blustered Dad, in total disbelief?

"I have a big fish on! Shut it off!"

Dad threw the throttle control across. Meanwhile, I concentrated on my fish, which had just risen to the surface.

POW! A gun shot echoed down the river.

My fish stiffened and rolled over. I looked up at Dad's eyes glaring over the still smoking rifle.

"We've wasted enough time!"

I didn't argue.

The engine started about one second after the thirty-inch fish hit the floorboards.

By the time we reached the east end of Tramping Lake, Dad's quiet demeanour had reasserted itself.

We had fish for lunch.

Spider Island

In our attempt to reach the Morton Lake Portage,
we had been island hopping since early morning.

Island hopping is the routine you use when attempting to
navigate long dangerous wind-swept stretches of open water.
You patiently wait until there is a small break in the wind and/or
waves, at which time you quickly nip out and run up into the
leeward of the next island or headland.

Our sixteen-foot square-sterned canoe pushed by the trusty
five-horse Johnson was no match for the three foot rollers.

It was about three o'clock when Dad made a long dash out
to a small island at the junction of the southern and western
arms of Reed Lake, where we tied up in a natural slip on the
northeast corner. We walked across to the west end for a better
look. There were no more islands, just miles and miles of open
angry white-capped water. It was profoundly obvious we had
progressed as far we could, and we would have to camp
overnight in the hopes of continuing in the morning.

We set up the tent in a lovely flat area behind the west end
tree line. With the campsite properly arranged, we explored the
island.

The island was somewhat rectangular, perhaps two hundred

feet by two hundred and fifty feet on an east-west strike. The entire west end was lined with a double row of large white spruce, which appeared as if they had been deliberately planted. Very little wind penetrated to the tent, which was only a few feet behind them.

To look at the shoreline below the trees was to envision a master builder at work, precisely placing large boulders at the waterline with progressively smaller rocks up towards the trees.

After commenting how this seemed to be the perfect campsite, we soon discovered vestiges of other campsites.

We nicknamed the south side The Orchard where stands of Birch and Poplar shaded Pin Cherry trees and Saskatoon bushes, while Blueberry bushes abounded with the bunchberries in the deep moss carpet.

A large flat rock on the southeast corner became the fishing spot from where Northern Pike and Pickerel were caught.

Along the east end an intertwined line of cedars and alders made it impossible to reach the water's edge.

All this was startling enough until we discovered why there were no flies, no bugs, and – best of all – no mosquitoes or black flies. The entire north side was one immense spider web.

The term 'spider web' does not adequately describe the enormity of this living entity.

The 'web' consisted of thousands and thousands of spiders and their webs all interlocked. From the waterline it stretched upwards for more than twenty, and was about two feet thick in some places. This massive network terminated at the spot we had landed.

During our three-night stay, we encountered only two

mosquitoes, both of which landed on Dad. The first one was killed instinctively, but the second one appeared to be so pathetically skinny, he let her fill up completely. When she finally withdrew her proboscis, she couldn't fly! We watched her stagger around and eventually fall off.

It was really funny.

The winds, which marooned us, never abated until sometime in the middle of the third night. There was nothing to do except eat, sleep, pick berries for the pancakes, catch and cook fish, relax and feed the few visiting mice which actually became quite tame.

In retrospect, I suppose, the best part of that impromptu confinement was that as a teenager, I was able to discuss things with my Dad that, under normal circumstances, would never have been explored.

During the following month, we did reach the Morton Lake Portage, but when out of curiosity, we swung by 'Spider Island', only a few wisps of the immense web remained. Although we entertained many theories regarding its destruction, the mystery remained.

Images of that monstrous web on Spider Island are as vivid today as they were almost fifty years ago.

Strung Out

"Well, here I go again," Andrew grumbled, as he started up the rope ladder. "Has to be more to life than walking an inch and a half diameter rope strung out some seventy feet."

It wasn't the sixty-foot height that irritated him. It was the fact that this state required a safety net. He had performed higher than this without a net! He was being treated like an amateur.

Thoughts of his new grandson crept in, the reality of which consoled him somewhat.

"Oh well, I suppose, it's better to be safe and alive to enjoy him," he smiled inwardly. "He needs his grandpa."

He was slightly out of breath when he reached the high-wire platform. "Maybe I can find something else to do, preferably on a level surface," he puffed. "I'm getting a little too old for this."

He disdainfully surveyed the usual crowd, squealing and clapping at the vanishing horses and elephants.

"At least, I don't have to clean up," he muttered.

The odour of fresh animal dung wafting upwards within the warm tent atmosphere reinforced his bias. "I really wish they would schedule me before that act," he cranked, "or, at least much later on."

But soon the acrid smell was replaced by a cacophony of more tolerable aromas from popcorn, hotdogs, straw, and the smoke from the clowns' cannons. The frenetic antics of the Bremmington Buffoons were designed to distract the audience from the cleanup squad.

"Won't be long now," he thought, scrubbing his special shoes in the tacky resin box. Meanwhile his skilled fingers kneaded the rosin bag. The audience would not see him check the rope tension with the experienced foot of a thousand walks or the practiced eye watch for that certain specific vibration.

From up on his darkened platform, he heard the circus band play the 'announcement' theme, with its familiar brassy crash. The audience din subsided as his friend Walter, the Ring Master, held up his arms.

'I wonder how his daughter is doing after her fall last night,' Andrew worried.

He stared at Walter. He always enjoyed this part.

"Ladies and Gentlemen. The moment you have all been waiting for is here. May I direct your eyes to the high wire," (The spot light momentarily blinded him as Walter continued) "to the Great Arlondo, King of the High Wire!"

Andrew pasted a smile on and waved at the audience. "You bunch of twits," he sneered through his smile. He grasped the rubbery handgrips on the balance beam. "If you only knew how simple it is to walk on this big rope, especially with a long stabilizing pole."

The band played the usual accompanying music that, theoretically, enhanced the danger. It was all well rehearsed and choreographed.

'I'm getting too old for this,' he thought as his feet moved with confident smoothness, the soles tracing every familiar ratty fibre. "Man, this rope is as tired and worn out as I am," he mumbled.

He lay down on the rope and dropped one leg down to enhance the stability. "And why not? We practically grew up together!"

After receiving the expected screams and squeals when he pretended to almost fall off, The Great Arlondo eventually hopped onto the opposite platform, glued on another look-at-me smile, and waved at his adoring fans.

While allowing the appropriate amount of time to elapse, his mind recalled earlier times when he did not need the beam, but conceded that Walter was correct to insist upon its use.

Leaving the pole there, Andrew picked up the skipping rope and proceeded out onto the wire. The routine was not particularly difficult. The trick was to make certain the tightrope did not oscillate at the same frequency as his skipping tempo. With the sequence completed, he returned to the platform and put the rope on its hanger.

The applause improved his mood.

He could almost taste his wife Maria's cabbage rolls.

Acknowledging the audience, The Great Arlondo, again became 'one' with balance beam. The return walk involved a series of skips, reverses and sitting down with the beam, on the rope. With the beam, it was a little harder on the buns, but it didn't last that long. Upon reaching the platform, he again waved to the cheering audience, as Walter announced "The Great Arlondo!"

The smile vanished as soon as the spotlight was redirected.

At the bottom of the ladder Walter was waiting for him.

"Are you alright, Andrew? You seemed to be a bit mechanical tonight."

"Yeah, I'm okay." He tried to sound upbeat, but he wasn't fooling his old friend. He was thinking of his grandson. Life had taken on a new priority.

Andrew attempted deflection. "How is your Sarah?"

"A bit bruised, but she will be back on her horses tomorrow," Walter answered, but it was obvious he had not been put off. Putting his massive arm around Andrew's shoulder he said quietly, "We'll talk tomorrow, my friend. Ok? Right now, I have some work to do."

Andrew could only nod.

He could smell the cabbage rolls and put on a happy face as he entered the trailer. His daughter Jenny was there with the grandson, but as he picked up the baby, he caught Maria's look. She knew something was bothering him.

Later that night they would probably go for a long walk.

The Survivor

The other day I chanced upon the scrawny longhaired grey-white cat I had met in early fall a few years ago. At the time he was just a kitten, and it looked as if someone had just tossed him out. When I approached him he was already quite wild.

This time I stepped aside as his whole aristocratic demeanour stated: "Don't bother me."

Watching him I remembered worrying if he would survive the coming winter, but when I saw him months later, he was endowed like a fluffy cloud and a very determined look.

I recalled thinking 'I should call the pound that would 'rescue' him.' but it was Saturday, and the place was closed.

So that was that.

Later on that week, an interesting coincidence occurred. A TV slot was dedicated to some animal welfare group, which wanted to chastise people who release unwanted pets into the streets. The programme explained how that particular group rescued these discarded pets and put them up for adoption.

Any viewer-sympathy they aspired to invoke was completely destroyed by the presentation.

The production took place in the shelter's operating room. After watching the programme, the only resemblance to the word 'shelter' meant that the roof didn't leak.

From among the innocent inmates a victim was chosen to be the 'star' of the macabre demonstration. The narrator, the assistant, droned on about, "The place becomes crowded and room must be made for more incoming animals. We do this by eliminating those who have outlived their adoptive time limit, which is two weeks."

(I cringed at the words: 'time limit'.)

The underlying inference was: 'If you are looking for a pet, you had better make your selection quickly otherwise it – and many others – dies.'

The other problem, I mused, was that today's society seemed immune to slaughtered pets, and does not see the need to criticize such procedures.

No one had come for the dog.

They did not mention if it had a name. The assistant laid perfectly healthy Golden Labrador Retriever upon the stainless steel table. The trusting face and wagging tail never showed any sign of resistance. So while the aide held the dog, the doctor injected a single syringe full of transparent lethal fluid.

The white-coated assistant never batted an eye. She stroked the dying head, looked into the camera and said, "I hope you all can see what happens things get overcrowded. Euthanasia is the only solution."

Did the assistant have any love for animals? Did she or the 'doctor' have any feelings of remorse?

I doubt it.

The unintentional point made was: Don't trust your outgrown dog or loving cat with the S. P. C. A. or similar facility.

The programme emphasized how cats were killed much

sooner than dogs! If it was meant to be a consolation, it wasn't. In fact, it was a poignant malediction!

I thought of all these things as I watched the cat. He didn't look any worse for wear. As a matter of fact, he looked much fitter than the last time I saw him. He had a confidential air and padded by as if he owned the place.

Well, that was five years ago and somehow he's adjusted to his lot in life. I have no idea where he lives. He patrols his territory, does not bother anyone, and minds his business.

One conclusion I could make: He has certainly lasted longer than with the animal shelters.

The Box

He touched the little box in his pocket and smiled.

'I'll fix her good.' Vengeful thoughts were racing through Jeremy's his head. 'She'll be sorry she made me do that stupid math question over and over again on the blackboard. She knows I have a hard time with multiplying. I was so embarrassed – especially with Susie watching.'

Jeremy fingered the elastic band holding the lid on as he remembered how some kids giggled as he continued through the question, as Miss Hill kept pointed out the mistakes he was making.

'I hate Grade Five.'

He visualized the huge spider – it must be an inch across – he had found yesterday and put into the small blue jewellery box. He'd drop it into that wide centre desk drawer – the one that was usually partly open – the one that held the register from which Miss Hill called out the names every morning.

Jeremy made certain he was one of the first ones through the main door when the bell rang, and headed for his classroom. His fingers flicked off the elastic, but as he entered the door his heart sank. The drawer was closed! Oh well, no turning back now. He withdrew the box, removed the lid and dumped out the spider, which skittered under some papers.

'Wow! Will she be surprised and scared!'

Finally Miss Hill came in and headed for her desk. As she pulled out the flat drawer, the spider emerged. Miss Hill made a little 'OH' sound and backed away. When the class saw it, there were squeals from the girls and faces on the boys.

"Would someone please remove that spider?" she said, looking around the room. "Don't kill it, as it is quite beautiful; just catch it and put it outside."

When nobody moved, Miss Hill looked at Jeremy.

"Jeremy," she stated softly, "You are the class naturalist, so you know how to handle such creatures. Would you please take the spider outside?"

Jeremy felt pretty good.

Inverting a glass over the spider, he carefully slipped a stiff paper under the rim.

Everyone, including Miss Hill, relaxed as he left the room.

Upon returning to his desk, Miss Hill gave him a lovely smile. "Thank you Jeremy. That was very brave."

Jeremy was very happy until he heard, "This morning we are going to continue with multiplication."

The Old Timer

Since mid morning I had been following a predetermined compass line towards a cragged hill, which according to the provincial geological survey maps, promised good prospecting.

Although it was hard going at times – encountering the many cross-path invisible sticky spider webs did not help – I thoroughly enjoyed the multitude of warning signals preceding me: the blue jays' harsh cry, the crows cackles, and the shrill chatter of the red squirrels' relay system as I entered each one's territory.

I especially preferred this particular time of year when the late August sun was not too hot and the season for biting insects was over although a few persistent whining irritants plagued my neck and ears, disregarded the repellent and somehow managed to discover an unprotected spot.

The colours were always fantastic. The crimson sumacs presented a stark contrast against the ochre carpet of deciduous leaves outlining the conifers.

Briefly closing my eyes to brush yet another web from my face, I was surprised to enter an open area, the brightness of which indicated it was an old cut. From the size and height of the white birches, with their ratty yellow leaves and the golden brown aspens, I estimated the region had been logged about thirty years previously.

The angle of sun told me it was close to one o'clock, so while visions of an anticipated lunch played in my mind, I failed to see a fallen branch. In an effort to stop my headlong fall my hand reached for and grabbed the nearest stabilizing feature which in this case, was a huge old stump. The sudden external pressure was too great for the frail old fellow, and a large piece of the deteriorated side crumbled and became part of my unceremonious crash.

Since I was unhurt, I laughed, relaxed, lay back and took time to enjoy the unexpected respite on the soft bed of moss and leaves exuding that wonderful bush smell I had grown to love. I also wondered if the chattering squirrel was laughing at me or sounding the usual alarm.

Looking up I discovered I was beside the remnant of a huge white pine, which quite likely had been cut over a hundred years ago. Although long dead it was still supplying security and nourishment to a couple of white spruce seedlings and a ring of alders. A layer of moss and lichens, displaying their miniature light-pink flowers on their pencil-line stems. The coating seemed to cuddle the stump in a cozy green-grey blanket out of which several large two-tone brown fan fungi emerged.

In my lap the large piece of rotten wood emitted that characteristic mushroom odour as it disintegrated in my hands.

I figured the stump would offer a convenient place to have lunch. When I stood up, I discovered I was not the only one that thought so, for there were thousands of discarded golden spruce cone flakes and cores covering the top, creating a four-foot amber mosaic upon a dark brown cracked backdrop.

Although inviting, the thin layer of dense jade moss still

held the previous night's rain and discouraged any thoughts I had of sitting down.

Perched on a fallen tree, I studied the old remnant while I munched my peanut butter sandwich. I was intrigued how much it resembled an ancient extinct volcano, for its soft central core had long ago disintegrated creating a jagged dark two-foot caldera, the bottom of which protected several red bunch berry plants nestling in a spongy bed of wood and leaf till.

The rustle of dry leaves distracted me. The squirrel and I saw each other at the same time, whereupon it dropped its spruce cone, scampered up the nearest tree and severely scolded me. I laughed, told him he could have the dining room table, and apologized as I put the last bit of my sandwich on the stump.

After a long cool refreshing drink from my water flask, I re-established my compass bearing. Then after swinging my packsack over my shoulder, I gently patted the old timer on its rough rotten top and told it to keep up the good work.

I think if I went back there today I'm certain I would find it fulfilling its destiny.

The Mystical Mirror Shard

It seemed as if it had always been there, its sharp thick triangular shape jammed into the darkened upper corner of the transit shelter.

During the morning rush commuters came to rely upon it to do last minute unobtrusive primping, and it was weird how a shiver would tingle down the spine if the scrutiny lingered.

But if the mirror was alone with a tarrying traveller, the mirror unleashed its mystical power, capturing the individual's mind with invisible tentacles.

The imposed consequence depended upon the person's heart condition. If the spirit were one of crushed honesty, the mirror would grant an unsaid wish and the encouragement to await its fulfillment; or if the person's life was being torn by conflicting influences, the mind was gently nudged towards an understandable resolution.

Should the mirror encounter a person concealing an evil exploitation of his fellow man, the glass would inflict such remorseful mental anguish, that the perpetrator would soon make amends and atone for the mistake.

Although it had initiated many positive measures through the years, the mirror never witnessed any results of its astonishing strategies. During quiet times, it brooded and wondered if it was worth the exertion.

One raw night, a gentleman entered the shelter, stood his umbrella in the corner, and was about to brush fluff from his overcoat when he noticed the shard. While using the reflection to tidy things up, he was surprised when a mist swirled across his image and it dissolved into a diorama.

In an office, a shocked man was explaining to the executor that his inheritance should have been much larger. When the client departed, the avaricious administrator could be seen gleefully enjoying his windfall.

Abruptly the scene changed, and showed the consequences of the crime upon the young family: the struggle for mortgage payments; the subsistence living; the loss of their home; and the constant stress, which led to their eventual break-up.

The scene returned to the office. Although the administrator had felt triumphant at the time, latent twinges of goodness had prevented him from spending the ill-gotten gains. In the hope of finding his client and setting things aright, he had put it into an annuity.

Busy business life often pushed these thoughts aside, but it was at night the dull insistent ache gnawed at him, depriving him of sleep.

Renewed regret wrenched the traveller's heart, but while continuing to stare through tear-blurred eyes, an unexplained excitement filled him, a feeling as if his yearning would soon be fulfilled.

Suddenly, the mirror cleared, leaving his surprised face gazing back.

The Route 20 bus hissed to a stop where the man fumbled for and deposited more than enough change for the fare. He scurried into a back seat and looked out into the night where the window reflected a face whose eyes showed the strange mixture of elation and apprehensiveness.

Nervous fingers felt for the umbrella.

He had forgotten it!

The tired irritated driver let the embarrassed passenger exit and disdainfully watched him hurry back to the original boarding point.

Meanwhile, a lone tired figure had seen the bus disappear, then shambled into the transit shelter to await the next one. The mirror watched him pull his worn long coat around him, and slink into the darkest corner, which offered some shelter from the damp evening breeze. It was obvious life had been mean, difficult and unforgiving.

Peering into the mirror, the stranger made a half-hearted attempt to straighten his wet stringy hair, and while he was looking at his scruffy baggy-eyed reflection, the mirror seized his mind.

The image misted then cleared to reveal a depiction of two gentlemen seated either side of an office desk, where a financial transaction was in progress. The taller man was explaining the various points of an important document.

The faces were indistinguishable, but from the body language and the gesturing, it was evident the shorter man was becoming visibly upset and disappointed in what was happening.

It was all vaguely familiar somehow.

The client picked up a package, shook hands with the sad-faced official, and slumped out of the room. Although the scene continued to be blurry, the administrator was suddenly, strangely happy, and pulled a handle to reveal a drawer filled with bonds and stocks.

The picture magnified the name on the sheets: It was his father's name!

Mirror then exposed the official's face. The poor man staggered backward when he saw that it was his trusted friend, Henry, who had been his father's executor.

His dad had been correct: there had been sufficient money to pay off the mortgage, with some left for investment.

He thought about his Jenny and how his little family had struggled to pay the monthly mortgage along with other necessities; how eventually the constant strain took its toll; and how the avaricious bank foreclosed, forcing his young wife to go home to her parents 'temporarily'.

Tears glistened, but at the same time, a strange exhilaration spread through him, as the mirror showed him holding his smiling wife and children.

The mirror went blank as the umbrella's owner came rushing into the shelter.

Recognition was instantaneous. Angry eyes met startled ones. Distrust bit into surprised relief.

Before the poor man could react, the other man had stepped forward, and grasped him by the shoulders.

"George! I'm so glad I found you! I've been looking for you for ages."

George tried to escape, hatred motivating every stiff movement.

Although Henry was somewhat taller, he seemed to shrink

under George's coldness. Cold steel-grey distrusting eyes stared back.

"I have wanted to make amends ever since I cheated you, but when I tried to find you but you seemed to have vanished."

The mirror shard smiled as George's confused mind tried to make sense of the flurry of words coming at it, vaguely hearing the words inheritance...annuity...apologize.

The man's eyes pleaded with George. Sincerity began to penetrate.

"It's all there, George. In fact, it's probably doubled in size." It was as if the other man could not confess fast enough.

His head dropped. "Believe me, George, I'm not the man I was. Please forgive me."

The man was a defeated shell.

Gradually, George grasped the reality of the situation. It was the resolution the mirror predicted. He glanced at the mirror, but saw only normal reflections.

The man's voice slowly penetrated George's thoughts.

Henry was rattling on about staying over night; explaining how he could call his wife; how it would be all right; that she wouldn't mind; that they could sort everything things out that very evening.

Somewhat embarrassed, George instinctively pulled his worn coat more tightly around him, explaining that he'd rather not.

Realizing George's awkwardness, the taller man apologized profusely, quickly rummaged through his pockets and produced a business card, which he eagerly thrust at George.

"Here, take my card," he said. "Can you meet me at my office tomorrow?"

George nodded, mumbling something about not having to go to work until three.

"Great! Wonderful!" The man brought out his wallet. "Here's a ten for bus fare. No, no. Here is thirty dollars for a cab. Please come by whenever it is best for you. I'll have all the documents ready."

Henry noticed George stiffen at the words, and put his hand gently on the other's shoulder.

"There will be no funny business this time, George." There was true sincerity in his voice.

George continued to nod.

The mirror smiled as Henry suddenly, impulsively hugged George, and then beamed into his face.

"I'm so glad I forgot my umbrella because look what else I found!" Slowly he lowered his gaze. "And I found myself too."

George was about to say 'I'm glad', but the man interrupted him.

"There's my bus!" he announced. "I'll see you tomorrow morning." With that, he was gone, leaving George staring at the three ten dollar bills.

The mirror watched as the enormity of the situation finally registered as the man moved under one of the shelter lights, extracted a picture from his ratty wallet, and with fingers, roughened by hard work, softly traced hid wife's pleasant features.

Gently tucking Jenny's picture back into the wallet, along with Henry's card, and the three tens, he with a certain decisiveness approached the mirror. From a small packet he took a tissue and with gentle, loving strokes cleaned the reflective face.

"Thank you," said the tear-stained image. "Thank you very much."

As the shard watched the man disappear, it was immensely pleased because it was the first time it had seen immediate results.

The shard settled back and happily awaited the next solitary person.

Are you harbouring some evil deed; something you wish you could rectify? Perhaps, someday in your travels, you will find yourself alone with the Mystical Mirror Shard. Do not resist. Give in to its pervasive persuasion. It only wants to help.

The Key Rack

Trouble? Let me tell you about trouble.

It all began when I bought a neat three-hook key rack, and showed it to my wife who was busy composing a website. I told her I wanted to put it up by the door of the apartment.

"That way, I'll know where my keys are."

When there was no reaction, I prompted, "I think I'll hang it up by the door."

"DO IT!"

I scurried off. When it was dangling from a small nail, I took my keys from their familiar spot in my pants pocket, and plunked them onto the middle hook.

Fine.

When I ventured down to the front lobby to pick up the newspaper, I discovered I had locked myself out. With some trepidation, I knocked on the door, and after some delay, and a second tap-tap, it opened.

"Heh-heh," I announced at my wife's departing figure, "I, um, locked myself out."

A little while later, upon returning from the storage room, I realized I had again forgotten my keys.

With as much bravado as a husband can muster in such an

inextricable situation, I knocked and called out, "Honey, I have, er, locked myself out again."

I thought by adding the 'again', it might help.

It didn't.

I had to wait longer this time, but eventually the door opened a crack. By the time I was fully inside, she was at the computer room door, where she paused, turned, looked directly at me, her gorgeous dark eyes flashing, and said in a tone which left little doubt as to its implications, "I have better things to do than opening that stupid door. If you can't remember your stupid keys, then hang the stupid thing OUTSIDE!"

Obviously, the word 'stupid' was not intended for the inanimate objects.

I crept into my chair where I hoped some television would offer a safer environment.

One news item, dealing with the increase in auto thefts made me wonder if I had locked the car. I nipped out to check. Upon returning to the lobby, I felt my heart hit my shoes. The keys were upstairs—-in the apartment—-on the rack.

"Oh, no!" I groaned.

I considered sleeping in the car. That idea was instantly negated, because the car keys were also up there.

I was doomed.

With shaking finger, I pushed the entry buzzer...just a little bit.

When she answered, I apologized profusely for disturbing her and slunk upstairs, expecting a well-deserved scolding.

I was relieved when she wasn't in sight, but soon discovered my keys on my chair, and the missing key rack in the trashcan.

I left it there.

What If.....

Tired of waiting for more attention, and noticing the flies were arriving, the cat rose, stretched, walked across the quiet form, and stepped onto the table. He sniffed the little cylinders, and then the machine into which the man had been speaking.

When the cat leaves, his paw depressed a small lever, which made the machine click, whir, and click again. The machine began talking.

I suppose it was bound to happen – insidiously – rapidly – silently – and with perfunctory decisiveness.

For the record, my name is Antonio – Antonio Malachi – not that it means a hill-of-beans to anyone, because I'm probably one of the few left alive in the entire world, which isn't much of a consolation prize.

I'm propped up in a lawn chair at some dude's fancy cottage – if you can call it a cottage – more like a mansion by a lake – has a swimming pool – even the lake wasn't good enough for this guy – maybe that's him disintegrating in it – who knows – I really don't care.

This is probably his cat – friendly fellow – likes his chin scratched, don't you – yes, you do – there – feels good, eh – I wonder if he knows how fortunate he is?

I'm glad the medicine cabinet had a few puffers – they certainly help my breathing – for now anyway.

A couple of harsh coughs are heard and a puffer's hiss.

That's better – you know, it too bad people didn't appreciate – *cough* – didn't appreciate the earth's fragile beauty.

Did you know a dragon fly rattles when it takes off? – And raven's wings go whoosh-whoosh? – And birds! There are all kinds of birds singing around me – birds whose names I wish I had learned.

But, it's too late – too late – everything is too late.

A puffer is heard again.

Not much longer now – coughing up blood, and the lesions are leaking – it's the last stage – so while there is still a bit of time, I will use this tape recorder to describe what happened – if only for my own piece of mind.

Although many theories were expounded as to why the pandemic affected only humans, its exact origin was never determined. Unsubstantiated rumours blamed everything from gene splicing to cloning to a virulent variant of the AIDS virus. The embroiled debacle of assigning responsibility swiftly degenerated into basic survival instincts. During the initial scramble to develop counter measures, the strain's extreme virulence killed the investigators faster than they could isolate it.

Time ran out – *cough* – Time simply ran out.

In the great urban centres, the infection spread easily. Martial law was declared, but it was totally ineffective because soon there were no marshals and very little law.

Within months, world governments collapsed; civilization deteriorated from simple looting to uncontrolled chaos. Suicide became the norm.

The multitude of 'temporary' crematoriums soon became permanent fixtures, but even those ceased to function due to the lack of operators – certainly wasn't from a dearth of prospective candidates."

A wry sarcastic laugh is heard, then coughing.

Ouch! It even hurts to laugh.

There is no one alive in the cities or any other centres, no matter how small – just well fed dogs, cats and rats – AND FLIES! Flies are everywhere – millions and millions of them – on the walls – on the streets – in great black pulsating clouds overhead. It's Nature's clean up crew at work.

A violent bout of coughing is heard, during which the narrator is heard spitting up some phlegm. Several hisses of a puffer are followed by a struggle for breath.

People escaping the city carried the disease to the more remote regions. In a desperate attempt at self preservation, small isolated villages turned themselves into wilderness fortresses, preventing contact with all outsiders. These, too, slowly became ghost towns where only the incessant buzzing of flies was heard.

Some paranoid individuals tried hoarding food, barricading themselves in almost inaccessible caves, and killing anyone who came near. But, the flies found them.

There might be some individuals scattered around the Arctic and Antarctic Poles, but they won't last long. The flies will find them – the flies find everyone.

Laboured gasping

I – I suppose, now that the human race is on the verge of extinction, the earth will return to the paradise it once was. Clear cut forests, fish stocks and the rain forests should regenerate fairly easily. Desertification will be reversed. Rectifying and repairing the oil spills and the tailings ponds abandoned by mining companies will take much longer, but it will happen – it will happen.

Another violent coughing fit is heard.

I wish I could watch this wonderful transformation – the earth reverting to its natural paradisiacal grandeur, where all life works in harmony – (a groan of agony is heard) – without man's interference.

It's ironic to think the only thing the earth didn't need is mankind.

What if we had heeded the signs?

What if we had not been so greedy?

What if we (a great painful moan) – got – what we – (gasp) – deserved?

A fit of violent coughing is heard, followed by a long sigh.

The machine fell silent.

Double Jeopardy

I felt empty and alone, while anger seethed within me.

It wasn't fair. Just when everything was coming together for him and his new family, my best friend, Barry, had been killed in bazaar hit-and-run accident.

Seeking solace after today's funeral, I retreated to an isolated section of the park, where the squeals of children and adult laughter seemed to add 'salt' to my spiritual wounds. Didn't they know? Didn't they care that one of the nicest fellows one could ever hope to meet was dead?

But how could they?

I was blankly staring between my feet – trying to make sense of the tragedy – when an ant appeared. With antenna rapidly surveying the area, she became focused on something straight ahead. I followed her gaze to see a rather large cookie crumb in the middle of the sidewalk.

'What a choice morsel,' I thought, 'if she could just reach it.'

The ant took a few steps, hesitated, advanced some more, and then boldly stuck out for her objective.

I cheered her on: 'Go, girl, go!'

She grasped the large crumb, turned, and headed back.

I whispered, 'Hurry up! Come on. Come on!'

A pair of trousers shattered my concentration.

"No!" I yelled, with sudden realization!

The ant lay crushed beside her prize.

Life personified!

I buried my face in my hands and cried for Barry and my ant.

Long Ago and Far Away

Date: OUA Time

Grassy Knoll,

Fantasy Farm.

Dear Wolf:

Thank you for your kind words regarding the Gingerbread Man. It certainly was a strange experience. I have my eye on the rooster that was at the end of the line. I hear you have moved into a new territory. What is it like?

Your friend,

Fox

Date: OUA Time

Jack Pine Corners,

Fantasy Forest.

Dear Fox:

My new digs are an extensive pine forest. I discovered an interesting little trail cutting through it. The south end leads to a little cottage where a sickly old female human putters around in a garden. A woodcutter working nearby comes for lunch in the early afternoon.

At the other end is another house where a younger female human lives, and there is a smaller one running around. I think that once I dispense with the red cloak and hood she always wears, she should be very tender. I'll keep you posted.

Cheers,

Wolf.

Date: OUA Time

Grassy Knoll,

Fantasy Farm.

Dear Wolf:

Please be careful. I have been told humans are quite tasty, but they can also be quite dangerous. Don't let that red outfit fool you. I suggest you carefully scout the place. Maybe there is a relationship between the two cabins that you can use to your advantage.

Awaiting your news,

Fox

Date: OUA Time

Jack Pine Corners,

Fantasy Forest.

Dear Fox:

Thank you for the idea. By watching and listening I have discovered that the old one is called a grandma and is usually sick. Periodically, the red-cloaked one takes a basket of food and goodies to her. I'll try to find out the schedule.

Till then,

Wolf

Date: OUA Time

Grassy Knoll,

Fantasy Farm.

Dear Wolf:

Sounds exciting! Please remember these little girls have a tendency to scream very loudly. Be careful. Didn't you mention there is a woodcutter around somewhere?

Worried,

Your friend, Fox

Date: OUA Time

Jack Pine Corners,

Fantasy Forest.

Dear Fox:

Guess what! The little girl has been taking the long way to her grandma's house! There is neat short cut that passes right by a cave in some big rocks where I could eat in peace!

Will write soon,

Wolf

Date: OUA Time

Grassy Knoll,

Fantasy Farm.

Dear Wolf:

I'm very happy and excited for you. I wish I could be there. But I was thinking about those rocks: a scream would echo off them. And I suppose the shortcut intersection is too open, eh? Have you considered using the Grandma's house to muffle the squeals?

Just suggesting,

Fox

Date: OUA Time

Jack Pine Corners,

Fantasy Forest.

Dear Fox:

What a great idea! I'll stuff the grandma in the closet, slip on one of her nightgowns and nightcap, and pretend I'm the sick one! Give me a few days to work out the details.

Till then,

Wolf

Date: OUA Time

Grassy Knoll,

Fantasy Farm.

Dear Wolf:

I think you are overlooking the fact that your ears, eyes, nose won't look at all like the Grandma's – especially your teeth! Perhaps another scheme would be safer? Just a suggestion.

Take care,

Fox

Date: OUA Time

Jack Pine Corners,

Fantasy Forest.

Dear Fox:

Don't worry, cousin, I'll just make up some excuses about how sick I am. Little girls always believe their Grannies. I'll write when my details are finalized.

Are you excited too?

Wolf

Date: OUA Time

Grassy Knoll,

Fantasy Farm.

Dear Wolf:

Sounds good. The old one should not be too much trouble. Just make certain you are quick and clean. You don't want the woodcutter to hear anything. Please write before you attempt your attack.

I'm worried.

Fox

Date: OUA Time

Jack Pine Corners,

Fantasy Forest.

Dear Fox:

It's all set for tomorrow! I saw the mom put the basket on the table for the morning. The kid usually picks some flowers near the short cut, so when I see her pass by, I'll nip down to the Grandma's and complete the transformation. I'll write and tell you how things went.

Wish me luck!

Wolf

Date: OUA Time

Grassy Knoll,

Fantasy Farm.

Dear Wolf:

I just had to write! I've been sitting here on pins-and-needles waiting to hear from you. Hurry up and give the news. I'll write again in a couple of days.

Please write soon.

Fox

Northern Manitoba Love

In the Northern Manitoba mining towns options for
dates are limited. It was in the summer that one pursued any
kind of meaningful relationship, and even then, you shared it
with the swarms mosquitoes and black flies.

During the brief summer one could go swimming, pack out
for lingering picnics, or take long walks. If things looked really
encouraging one hopped in the boat and found a private spot on
the lake.

I saw Nola during the Christmas holidays. She was new in
town, and hung out at her dad's hardware store. She didn't seem
to do very much. That didn't matter. Every day, I made some
pathetic excuse to go in, just to sneak a peek at her.

She was all a chap could wish for. She was taller than I was,
slim, and supple, with clear green eyes. I don't think she knew I
existed. I didn't care. I would wait until early summer before I
attempted to take her out.

Finally, on a Saturday in late June, I said, "Today's the day."

Since there was no hurry to come home, I put in extra gas in
for the five-horse outboard engine; packed a good lunch; and
finally I put her in the boat along with my dog.

It was wonderful. We spent the whole day fishing together.

With her Shakespeare casting reel, fifteen-pound braided
nylon line, and supply of hooks, she never once let me down.

An Ancient Appetizer

Long ago, in gentler times, Fox hurried to Wolf's house.

"Hey, Wolf," laughed Fox, rushing in and shaking his friend's shoulder and awaking him from his afternoon nap. "You're not going to believe what just happened."

Wolf blinked awake and mumbled, "Probably not, but I'm sure you're going to tell me."

Fox seemed to have trouble knowing where to begin.

"You know how I like to take my afternoon nap on that grassy knoll."

"Yeah."

"There I was, all snuggled down ready to doze off, when I heard this irritating refrain: 'Run, run, as fast as you can; you can't catch me; I'm the Gingerbread Man.' Well I couldn't sleep with all that racket, so I sat up and looked across the field towards the old farm. I can see pretty far from my look-out knoll."

"It's a good place to watch for danger all right."

"Well, away across the field, I see this line of critters running after a little brown thing, but I couldn't quite make out what it was. Anyway, there was a cook and her husband, followed by a horse, a cow, a dog, then a cat, and at the back, flapping like crazy, was a rooster!"

Wolf scratched sleepily.

"Are you sure you weren't dreaming?"

"No! No! And I could hear that silly ditty – Run, run, as fast as you can – over and over and over."

"From them?"

"No! From the Ginger Bread Man!"

"A Ginger Bread Man?"

"Yes."

"Now, I know you were dreaming," smiled the wolf.

"Honest! The whole gang was chasing him."

"Why?"

"I don't know, probably because he was teasing them. The next thing I knew, the little guy came to the river, stopped, turned and headed in my direction. So guess what I did?"

Wolf shrugged.

"I ran down by the old oak and waited till he came nipping along. As soon as he saw me, he began dancing around saying that stupid rhyme."

"And what did you do?"

"Nothing."

"Nothing?"

"Not a thing. In fact, I agreed with him."

"And then he left you alone." It was more statement than question.

"No! He became very angry. He said, 'You have to chase me.'"

"I said, 'No, I don't.'"

"Then he says, 'Every body has to chase me.'"

"So I said, 'Well, find someone else. I'm too full from lunch.'"

Wolf could see Fox was reliving every moment.

"Suddenly he hears the others coming, see, and he says, 'I have to get across the river.'"

"So I said, 'I'll take you across.'"

"And he says, 'No! You'll eat me.'"

"Naw,' I said. 'I told you, I'm full.'"

Fox leaned closer to Wolf's ear, and grinned. "I didn't tell him I had missed my dessert."

"'Climb onto my tail,' I said, 'and I'll swim across.'"

"'Well, alright', he says, 'But please keep your tail up.'"

"So, he climbed on and I started across, see, but pretty soon my tail started to get wet. So I said, 'You'd better climb onto my back where it is a little drier.' I could tell, even there, he was getting a little damp. I could feel him inching up my back until he was perched between my ears."

"He was happy and said, 'This is much better.'"

"'Yes, it is!' I yelled, and I flipped him up into the air and swallowed him down."

"You ate him!"

"Yup, in one gulp," Fox laughed. "I love ginger bread, especially when it is delivered fresh to the doorstep. And that's just the way it happened. Crazy, eh?"

Wolf nodded, and thoughtfully stroked his chin.

"So, Wolf, how's your day been?"

"Funny you should ask," said Wolf, rubbing the back of his neck, "because just a while ago, I met a little girl wearing a red cloak and red hood."

Kim's Game

Harvest days, when the warm wind-blown chaff-dust scratched his eyes, coloured Jeremy's dreams as the musky odour of old straw invaded his senses. The vision vanished when a sharp pain seared through his head, awakening him instantly. Gradually he realized his face was pressing into a hard musky gritty surface.

His eyes hurt when he opened them; at least he thought they were open because he could see nothing.

When he rolled onto his back, his reflexive 'OUCH' resonated hollowly. His fingers gingerly touched the spot where the pain centralized to find his matted hair matted and stiff. Memories of the past few hours – or was it days – must be hours – otherwise the wound would be a lot drier – slowly returned.

He had surveyed the darkened area before going to his car, but when he opened the door...

They must have been hiding in that other parked car.

The attempt to sit up made him nauseous, so he stayed on his back to figure out where he was. The absolute silence intensified the darkness – almost tomblike he thought wryly. High above was a faint halo of light. His hands gingerly explored what appeared to be a concrete floor, his now sensitized fingers feeling the tiny cracks under crunching crumbling grains and strewn straw.

Conscious of not moving his throbbing head too quickly, and pushing with his heels and elbows, he slid himself along the gritty floor until his head thumped against a wall. Ignoring the pain, and puffing from exertion, he pushed himself into a sitting position, while his hands discovered a curving corrugated steel wall.

Near the floor, almost directly across from him, was another faint rectangular light.

He realized he was in a grain bin.

A multitude of questions sprang to mind. Would they be back? How long had he been here? Was he was expected to die in here?

Well, he wasn't going without a fight.

When he reached for the shoulder holster, he knew his gun would be gone, but he was hoping they had missed the stiletto secreted behind it. He smiled as he felt its narrow hilt. He left it there, but he derided himself when he recalled buying the complete outfit for 'protection'.

"Great protection," he sneered inwardly. "Well, at least I'm alive."

The best offence was a planned defence. He had to see what this place offered in the line of weaponry. His finger searched for, and retrieved the penny matches from his back pocket. He opened it and put the matches against his cheek, knowing that if they felt cool, they were probably damp. He grinned when they had that nice smooth fine-sandpapery feel. His fingernail verified their hardness.

Great. Step one was complete.

Knowledge was strength, and he was feeling stronger by the minute.

In order to see what was inside the bin, he would have to plan the next step rather precisely, otherwise there was a good chance of asphyxiating himself.

On his knees and facing the outline of the door, he carefully scraped around until he had a small pile of straw in front of him; then visualizing exactly what he was doing, he ripped off a match, felt for the strike strip, folded the match cover over the head, and pulled.

Tiny as it was, the flash temporarily blinded him. Squinting through the pungent phosphoric smoke, he dropped the little flame onto the miniature haystack, which immediately caught fire. He quickly scanned the dimly lit interior.

It was apparent the bin had not been used for some time. Coughing and ignoring the acrid taste, Jeffery played Kim's Game, memorizing various objects relative to the door.

Snatching up a small handful of straw, he lit it from the dying fire, and held it as close to the latch side of the door. With his cheek rebelling at the heat, he tested the amount of play between the door and the frame, and estimated the width between the various sections.

A barely discernable shaded section along the narrow line of light indicated the location of the external latch.

The flame went out, making it seem darker than when he first became conscious.

Resting against the door, and enjoying the sweet odour of burned straw around him, Jeffrey began to prepare the next operation, the urgency of which depended upon whether they were coming back. Right now the priority was to assemble 'weaponry'. Following that, he would try to escape.

From his reference point, and tasting the dry muskiness he was stirring up, Jeffrey crawled around collecting his inherited treasures. The tin can with its ragged lid was put with the axe head. A short piece of reinforcing rod went beside the broken harrow hook. He put the coat hanger and the baling wire near the door. Lastly, he scrambled over to the small pile of scrap steel, and thought about raccoons as his fingers probed, then selected, a very thin flat piece.

His shoe crushed the can so that the attached lid became a circular blade. The coat hanger was shaped such that when he grasped it, its long straightened hook extended between his middle fingers, making it perfect for a throat lunge.

The harrow hook, piece of rod, and axe head could be effective missiles.

Finally, pleased with layout of his meagre arsenal, he leaned back against the doorway. With thoughts of revenge making his jaw muscles clench, he began bending the thin iron strip at precise memorized lengths to fit around the doorframe near the outside latch.

There was only one nagging question: would he have enough time?

Lakeside Departure #1

Horace was fagged out. At his age, it was normal to be tired, but this morning – this particular morning – he was feeling downright plumb tuckered out, and the tightness in his chest did not help the situation.

His shaking hand clasped the park bench as he, gasping and wheezing, eased himself onto his bench, which was the one nearest the water fountain. It was also the intersection to the many park paths. It wasn't really 'his' bench, but through time there came to be an unspoken law that reserved that particular spot for Harold.

He had not felt well since the morning when he forced himself out of bed, hurried to the park, there to maintain his daily self-imposed schedule of sitting by the pond from late morning till well into the evening. It was there he enjoyed the comparative peace while watching ducks, geese, pigeons and visitors who were absorbed in their respective worlds.

He berated himself for rushing so but he rationalized that the people expected him to be there, there on Harold's Throne.

Many folks knew him by name and enjoyed engaging him in conversations ranging from astrophysics to farming, from genetics to geography. Often the philosophical discussions he inspired made them late for work. They would laugh, hurry off, and vow to return tomorrow to continue the debate.

In his haste, he had forgotten his sandwich, but that was okay because Pete and his food cart would soon be along. Lately, Pete had begun refusing payment saying it was his treat, but Harold insisted upon paying for the ice cream bar. When Pete returned later in the evening, it was the same routine.

Another constant in Harold's life was the Mounted Police Patrol team of Constable Laurie McPherson and Constable James McKinnon who always managed to spend a few minutes with him while their horses drank at the fountain. If it happened to be later than usual, they would escort him home.

Because many major dialogues took place at lunchtime, people often shared their lives as well as their lunches. To them, he was their confidant, their counsellor and their grandpa. Although he never told anyone what to do, he easily discerned the root of their problems, and tactfully steered anxious individuals onto corrective courses. There were many evenings, with his heart aching from numerous desperate personal histories, Harold would shuffle off to the boarding house where he would fret all night, hoping he would meet the same anonymous folks in the near future.

The day at the lake followed the same pattern, but today Harold was increasingly edgy and irritated with himself. He found it very difficult to maintain a coherent conversation. People arrived with eager smiles, only to excuse themselves shortly thereafter, and leave with quizzical looks on their faces. When asked if he was all right, Harold, with a wave of his bony hand and his almost toothless smile, assured them he was just very tired today.

He was surprised how late it was when the park lights came on, but told himself that he would just have to wait until the internal heaviness eased up.

Staring out across the pond, Harold smiled weakly as some ducks sliced through the moon's reflection making, he surmised, a perfect image with which to close the day.

He took a deep breath, sighed, and hoped a short nap would help.

He did not hear the clip-clop of the horses that stopped in front of him. He did not see the tears from Laurie. He did not hear Constable McKinnon call the coroner's office.

Abandoned

To me, the little dwelling was the epitome of hard work, closeness and hominess.

Having spent an hour or so, prowling through the small, long-abandoned house, I re-entered the little white living room, and sat on a ratty old chair beside a homemade table.

'Well, that was interesting.' Resting my elbows on the table, and listening to Liz prowling around upstairs, I realized this room was noticeably different.

'It's strange how other rooms have at least one picture, whereas this one, almost deliberately, has none; just the outlines. If the walls could talk, what tales would they tell?'

The question had no sooner formed, than a great cold loneliness enveloped me. I looked around, half expecting to see someone standing there.

The squeaking staircase, signalling Liz was on the way down, interrupted the thought. I shook off the sensation, righted another chair, ensured its stability, and set it on the other side of the table.

"Whoever owned the place must have had at least two kids," she announced, swinging into the room, and sitting down. "Two little girls, I figure."

"Did you notice the built-in shelves under the beds?"

"Yes and that must have saved space in that low room."

"I liked the way that little closet angled into the end wall. There was a lot of love put into building it," I said, imagining all the time, patience and skill that must have gone into it.

"I wouldn't know," she said. "I do know there are still two little handmade dresses in it."

"And how about those stairs tucked in behind the pantry wall, almost like a hidden staircase."

I glanced around when I again felt that cold sense of abandonment.

"I wonder why they left." I asked, more to myself than Liz.

"Maybe they needed a bigger place."

"No, I don't think so," I said. "This place was perfect. They would have added on, probably to the north, off this room."

I glanced at her. It was obvious she didn't care.

"I wonder how old this place is," she mused.

"Well, it's not a log cabin, but the next best thing. The timbers and planking are pretty rough. Perhaps they could only afford so much, and did the most with what they had."

"That makes sense. Did you notice there are no doors on the rooms? They probably had a curtain on the adults' bedroom."

"Openness would have made for better heat circulation."

Suddenly overcome with internal melancholy, I shivered and thought, 'There is great disappointment here. The house is lonely. It is crying out in pain.'

Liz interrupted my thoughts. "That is probably what those rectangular cut-outs are for," said Liz pointing at the neat holes above the two doorways.

"You could be right," I commented, but my heart wasn't into the conversation.

"The warm air would circulate better, which is why the hole from the kitchen is bigger than the other one."

"Yeah, probably," I mumbled.

"And that small grate in the kitchen ceiling would let some warm air go upstairs."

"Mmmmm."

"And, of course, she would have a wood-burning stove for cooking and baking, in the corner where the big piece of tin is."

"Probably," I muttered.

"I think she hung her pots and pans on the walls."

"Could be." The coldness was intensifying.

"Are you listening to me?" Her angry tone startled me.

I looked straight at her. "Don't you feel anything?"

"No. Like what?"

"Oh, I don't know." I was at a loss for words. "Don't you get a strong sense of depression; of loss, of disappointment, of, of emptiness?"

"Of course, it's empty."

"That's not what I meant."

The sensation vanished, and my mind cleared. I blinked at the surroundings.

"They were pretty resourceful," I stated. "That pump by the kitchen sink goes to a cistern in the basement."

"I don't think they used that water for drinking. Probably used it for washing dishes and stuff," she said pensively.

"That was a pretty neat system they devised for diverting rainwater into it. Must have saved a lot of trips to the well."

"It should have been all right if they boiled it."

She was still thinking about the kitchen water.

"It was probably used for the livestock they kept in the cellar," I added. "I wonder what they had."

"Probably a cow, for the milk."

"Or a goat."

"Maybe a pig. It's easy enough to feed."

"Those box-shelves along the back by the window look like they were for chickens."

"Which would mean eggs."

"And roast chicken," I smiled.

"They could have used the feathers for stuffing pillows or quilts."

"Hard to say; all I know is there are two large stalls and one smaller one, which looks more like a pen."

"Whoever heard of keeping animals in a basement," said Liz, making a face.

"It never caught on in this country, but I know, in some European countries, it was – maybe still is – standard practice. Switzerland is one example."

I remembered it was while I was in the cellar, that I first became aware of a distinct internal sadness, but discounted it to the fact I was in a basement.

Lonesomeness was invading my mind again. I suppressed it somewhat.

"That large outside door probably allowed the animals come and go inside a fenced area."

"It must have smelled, with all those animals down there!" Liz's nose was in sync with her imagination.

"To a degree, I suppose, but if they kept it clean, it was probably alright."

"Yeah. But still..." Liz let it hang there.

"And the heat from the animals would have added some warmth to the house."

"That's a thought." Liz perked up. "It would be like live central heating."

We retreated inside our own thoughts.

"It's too bad," she mused, "They had to go outside to tend to the animals."

"No, they didn't," I said. "There's a trap door in the pantry, with a small ladder going down."

I shivered involuntarily, as once more a great sorrow tightened around me.

The walls reverberated my thoughts.

Fighting off another wave of wretchedness, I said, "That bedroom doesn't have much space other than for a bed and perhaps a small dresser."

"I don't think there was a dresser," stated Liz. "It looks like the bed also sat on a bunch of drawers."

When the conversation temporarily halted, the sense of melancholy instantly set in.

I stared at the walls. One moment, they gave evidence of a close hardworking couple; then suddenly, they exuded a great feeling of frustration and loss.

I desperately shook it off.

"The Hydro must have come in some time after they were settled," I stated, "Judging from the single light fixture hanging down in the middle of each room."

"The wife must have enjoyed that."

"Perhaps," I pondered. "But, I wonder if it contributed to the disintegration of this happy home."

"Now, how can you draw a conclusion like that?"

"It just came to me. But, if you look around, all the love and hard work seemed to have happened before Hydro."

"But electricity would have made things much easier."

"Would it?" I challenged. "Did it?"

"Certainly."

"And how would they have paid for it?"

"Oh, I don't know," she said, in a sombre tone. "Sell something, I suppose."

"And just what would they have to sell?"

"Weeeell…" Liz paused.

"Everything they needed was right here! They had worked for years to establish their own self-sufficient world. The house was their life. It gave heat, love, sustenance and protection. The Hydro ruined everything."

"What…?'

"She wanted some appliances."

Liz was staring at me.

"He wanted an electric pump!"

"How do you…?"

"He had to find odd jobs to pay for the extras. The little farm became neglected."

"What are you talking about?"

"When they sold the animals to pay for the Hydro, she had to start working for the neighbours in order to buy groceries."

"Where do you get…?"

"Pretty soon the house was just a place to sleep in."

The coldness intensified. My own agitated voice startled me. I had no idea where the words were coming from. It was as if the walls were speaking through me.

"Harry! Stop it! You're scaring me."

The tension vanished.

"Sorry, dear, I don't know what came over me. It was as if I could see the entire history of this house."

She continued to stare.

"Something quite unforeseen – insidious in its innocence – had destroyed this happy home."

I caught Liz giving me a curious, a rather worried look.

I made a feeble attempt to change the subject.

"Er, I didn't see a bathroom," I said, probably a little too loudly. "I saw an outhouse by the tree line."

"Maybe they used a sort of indoor port-a-pot," she smiled, but still had a worried look.

"I doubt it."

"But, what about cold weather?"

"I still think they used the outhouse, but they certainly would not have read the newspaper out there."

"I guess not," said Liz, getting up. "Well, shall we go?"

"Yeah, I suppose so," I said reluctantly.

As I stepped into the afternoon sunshine, I looked back into the lonely little house.

'If walls could talk,' I thought, 'What would they tell me?'

The words flashed into my mind: Please come back some day, if only for a little while.

A Slice of Life

Henry stared blankly at the remains of the pie and mused how life was like a homemade apple pie – or peach – or blueberry – or in this particular case, pumpkin.

He had cut another thin slice with full intention of enjoying another piece, but now thinking about his grandson, his fork randomly poked patterned holes across its surface.

His appetite had vanished.

It was just this morning, he and Robert had been laughing and talking as they shared their favourite dessert. Now with the opposite chair barren, his little apartment had again become a huge empty cavern. That precious ember that occasionally blew in and sparked his life had returned home in time for school.

Henry's melancholy mood made him philosophical. His life – for that matter anyone's existence – could be represented by that pie.

When first baked it signified the future: full and ready to be tasted.

The early years were akin to the first partitions when great expectations are heartily consumed.

As maturity seasoned the soul, the wedge size decreased, as less is required to satisfy an aging heart. Eventually, the remainder symbolized the unknown — the continually shrinking — timeline.

Gently, tenderly, Henry returned the pockmarked slice to the pan.

He stared at his grandson's picture on top of the television. His eyes blurred as he wondered how many more slices he had left.

The Old Artist

Long ago and far away in a small mountain town lived a well-beloved artist whose creations had a special magical quality. The painter seemed to extract part of the scene and put its life into the picture. When viewed the paintings exerted a strange affect upon each observer's mind.

"I can smell flowers."

"I hear birds."

"It's like I can feel the wind."

Admirers from all over came to see the master at work. When they would offer to buy his canvases, the artist would discern their hearts and only sell to those with pure intentions.

The village was very proud of their celebrity. Each day some would quietly gather around his easel where – they said – they felt they became part of the picture, which was often was completed in one day.

The artist staunchly refused to paint portraits, and the folks respected his wishes. When visitors persisted, friends would gently but firmly move them away so that the frail painter was insulated from such annoyances.

It also so happened that in the same town lived a wealthy but very irritating man who thought he could buy anything or anybody. He never seemed to have a kind word for anyone. He was tolerated by the townsfolk and reluctantly accommodated at the various shops.

He envied the artist. Many times he had attempted to purchase a picture only to be told it had been promised to someone else. Every day he badgered the artist to do his portrait – that no price was too high. The elderly painter always politely but resolutely declined.

As the years passed, the rich man's hatred towards the artist grew. Although they never directly spoke to the man, the people became more impatient with him and his irritating manner.

One year, during another long beautiful summer, the people noticed that it was taking much longer for the old artist to complete a masterpiece. Quite often it was only partially done when he began packing up. Knowing he would return, the townsfolk would help carry his materials back to the studio.

Usually the old artist came back the next day, but this particular summer, it might be a day or two before he reappeared, much to the people's relief. But as soon as the painter appeared, the angry rich man kept persisting upon having his portrait done.

One day when the artist arrived, he looked extremely drawn and frail. It was almost an effort to set up the easel, the chair and materials. Although the townsfolk were understandably worried, they quietly watched in case he needed something.

Once again, the arrogant man ignored the artist's fragile condition, and lashed out, "Why won't you do my portrait?"

The painter's tired voice rasped, "Have you never noticed

how the paintings captures the life in the landscape? Perhaps the same thing would happen if I painted a person. I can't take the chance."

"I don't care!" raved the man. "Don't you know who I am? I am very important around here. I must have my picture done so people will remember me."

The painter's ebony eyes blazed as he rasped, "A person is remembered for his deeds, not because he is frozen in time and space." The last words were spoken with an underlying warning – almost a threat. "Please leave me alone as right now, I don't feel very well."

"But I must have my portrait done! You have to do it."

"Very well," said the feeble voice, "Since you insist, come around to my studio tomorrow morning."

The man was excited. "I'll be there bright and early."

"Not too early," grinned the artist, "As I am old and need my rest. Just remember I cannot be held responsible for the result."

The next morning after the rich man was ushered into the studio, a DO NOT DISTURB sign was hung on the door. The people were glad that at last 'their artist' would finally be rid of the conceited impudent overbearing man.

A few days passed. After a week the townsfolk began to worry and asked the local constabulary to investigate – to make sure the old artist was all right.

Inside they discovered the old artist cold and stiff on his bed, and concluded he must have died peacefully in his sleep.

On the easel was the portrait of the angry wealthy man. Everyone marvelled how realistic he appeared.

"I can almost hear him yelling as usual."

"I think I can hear him swearing."

"I thought I heard, 'Let me go.'"

Not wanting to put the painting on display, the people put the angry painting in the museum's warehouse.

The town held a majestic funeral for their artist.

The rich man was never seen again.

Nobody missed him.

The Mystery
of the Misty Maiden

"Look," **said** **the** **real** **estate** **agent,** attempting to disguise his frustration when he saw Jeremy's eyes stray out the window to the cliff where the old abandoned house overlooked the sea. "Ye dinna want that place. The wee Murphy place down by the docks would be perfect — and a good price she is."

Jeremy slowly nodded. "It is a lovely place, but it's not quite what I have in mind."

"Well then, kin ye tell me again wha' ye be looking for?"

Jeremy stared past the gentleman with whom he had spent much of the cool misty morning investigating the few listed properties, and wondered how to explain ambience to one of these resourceful people who scratched out a living along these remote shores of northern Scotland. How do you explain, that after two fairly successful books, he had not written anything worthwhile in over three years, and his publisher was beginning to lose patience?

When extensive travelling and teaching had not worked, he had decided to try some self-imposed therapy, and had journeyed to this specific small village in the hopes to find isolation and inspiration.

"George, I apologize for being such a pain," Jeremy began. "The Murphy place, as you call it, is cute and picturesque and all, but I would like a place with real character." His eyes drifted back to the cliff. "I need a place where I can be alone."

In the town's only small café, he was instantly conscious of the other patrons glancing at him.

George leaned back, intertwined his fingers behind his head, and in a voice meant to be overheard, stated, "Well now, lad, ye no want that place for sure,"

Chairs automatically turned towards him when he said, "Why not?"

The agent grinned at the few customers around him. "He certainly won't be alone there, will he, lads, 'specially with The Maiden floating about?"

The lunchtime crowd was quite eager talk about the local haunted house and the Mysterious Misty Maiden.

"Well, may I at least have a look at it?

"Aye, that you can, but you can't buy it.

Why not?

You'll just turn around and give it back.

Because of what's-her-name, the Misty Maiden, I hear so much about.

Aye, she'll chase you out.

Well, it's a lovely day for walk; can't be much more than a half a mile.

True, but the climb will make it feel like two.

Have any of the villagers ever seen her?

Ach, no, not lately. Old Chester did a long time ago.

Would you introduce me to him?

Aye, that I would, lad, but he died three years ago – and a fine chap he was.

Anyone else?

Just those who tried to buy the house, but when they take back their small deposit and leave, I have no idea where they go. That's why I don't advertise it any more. No point, you see.

How about someone who might want to rent it?

Don't know – never tried.

Man, this is some hill. Let me catch my breath. This heath is not the easiest stuff to walk in, let alone going up hill.

Ach, you city folk are used to your sidewalks.

You're right. My, it certainly is gorgeous up here. I love the way the purples and mauves outline the deep blue of the firth.

And kin you smell it?

The ocean? Sure. There is always the smell of the sea around.

Ach, no: the heath.

I can't smell anything."

T'is not a strong odour, lad, but more like a wisp of a feather that flows o'er the moor, and brushes against your nose.

Well, let me try. You know, it is very faint, certainly not one to jump out at you.

Aye, that's it all right. And now no matter how far you roam, it will always with you.

I can see why you love it here. Are you a fisherman too?

Used to be, but me sons took over when I hurt me hand – couldn't pull the nets anymore.

Is that why you went into real estate?

That just happened when me brother was transferred to Edinburgh, he asked me to look after things, and that was more 'n twenty years ago.

Well, you certainly know...

Shhh! Look over there.

Where?

Just to the left of that dark clump of dark brown, there is a covey of quail.

I can't see anything.

Patient, lad, and you will see the heath move.

Yes! My goodness, they blend right in.

I suppose we should be moving along. Me Mary is expecting us for dinner.

I was kind of you to put me up for a few days while I looked for a quiet place for writing.

Have you been writing very long?

Oh, about ten years now.

Is it hard? What I mean is, hard to make a living at it?

Well, at times it's easier than climbing this hill.

I warned you.

I know. Oh, I've had a few things published – enough to keep me fed – starving artist and all that.

Well, here we be.

It's huge! It certainly didn't look this big from your place. Look at that balcony.

T'is a grand structure to be sure.

Have you ever considered turning it into a museum or tourist attraction?

Aye, it was 'considered' but we were afraid she wouldn't let us. The Misty Maiden.

Aye. Strange things happen when the house is involved.

Who built it?

Records indicate the garrison under General Stanton did. It was here long before I arrived, and probably before anyone else settled here.

There has to be a story behind this.

Well, the short version is that the crown sent a garrison into the firth to guard this side of the peninsula. While waiting for orders – which never came – the commander wanted to give the men something to do. So he had them design and build this house, using what materials they could find, plus the timber from one of the ships, which had run aground. The tiller is on the living room wall. You will see it though the window as we come around to the front.

Magnificent workmanship. I love the way the balcony overlooks the bluff. I thought you said nobody lives here.

That's right lad.

Well, it looks like a squirrel family has set up house keeping behind that hole under the eaves.

Aye, and there are probably quite a few other critters about.

Whoa! It's a long way down there.

Careful; these sea cliffs are very unstable.

I can see that.

That's what happened to her.

'Her' who?

The Commandant's wife.

He brought his wife out here!

Well, you see, when the house was done, the commander sent for his wife. They say she was quite the fair face.

It must have been a bit lonely, you know, no other ladies around.

I heard a few women came in later when nothing much was happening.

I'm amazed these windows haven't been broken.

Oh, apparently, they were once, long time ago. But something terrible happened to the vandals — which might have be pure coincidence — but no one could explain why. Ever since then, no one has dared harm the place.

I knew I could smell a story. Tell me more about the lady.

Well, they say she was wondering around one misty night and fell down the cliffs into the sea.

How awful!

But, they never found her body.

I'm not surprised.

You don't understand, lad. A body in these waters doesn't just 'disappear'.

It could have washed out to sea — currents and all that — fish.

Records show the tide was coming in at that time.

So, she would have gone that way, towards town.

Aye lad, towards the camp.

So, what happened?

Apparently, there was an investigation. Her husband was cleared and the case was closed, but soon after that he was replaced — due to stress you understand.

Understandable; he must have been shaken up losing his wife like that.

A few years later the entire garrison was recalled. That was the official story anyway.

Official story? Sounds like you don't believe it?

There was rumour that she was — shall we say — fraternizing.

And was she?

There was no evidence presented,

Which doesn't really answer the question, does it?

No, although it was noted the Commandant was extremely angry at times.

There is a story here. Have you heard the expression: when a rumour persists, there is usually an element of truth in it.

Aye.

What's this little enclosure?

That covers the little spring, which is fed by the upland rains – one of many throughout this region. I suppose that is one reason the house was built here. Watch out you don't – ach, too late, lad – I was going to warn you about the soft spots.

That's okay. Is that ever cold!

The commandant has a pipe laid from this spring to a cistern in the cellar, with an overflow pipe extending to the cliff.

Good idea, otherwise the place would be flooded out. So he was more than just a soldier.

Aye, bit of an engineer he was. Those are the kitchen windows looking east to catch the morning sun.

And that is quite a chimney, for the kitchen fireplace I presume.

Shall we go in? I've got the key here somewhere.

I would have liked to have met the person who carved the designs into this door! And look at these hinges!

The garrison's blacksmith probably made them. There we are – in you go, lad.

Doesn't that creaking door just set the mood somehow? It's gorgeous – like stepping back a hundred years! And no one wants to live here?

Oh, they want to. She won't let them.

By 'she' you mean the Misty Maiden.

Aye.

Angus, is there some connection between the ghost and the commandant's wife, you are not telling me about?

Well now, lad, you've heard that when a spirit continues to roam, it means a wrong has not been righted.

Yes, I've heard that.

So, why do you suppose the lady keeps appearing?

Maybe it wasn't an accident.

Aye, but I understand it was a cold rainy night when she vanished.

But you said no body was found.

Aye.

So, maybe she didn't drown?

Aye.

Which means she could be – still – here.

Now, you're getting the idea.

She could be right under our feet. Goodness. Look at the workmanship in this floor!

Considering the tools they had to work with.

You certainly couldn't sneak up on anyone around here.

This pump by the sink still works, although you would probably need to prime it a bit from this can here. You always filled the primer-can first before you did anything else.

Good habit. And the fireplace looks like it's hardly been used.

The whole house is like that. The dining room is through there, and this is the living room.

It's like a miniature dance hall! This furniture looks brand new.

Aye, it is. The folks just left everything.

And there's the tiller you mentioned.

And the ship's bell.

And another fireplace! This one is much larger than the other one. Angus, look at this. There seems to be a fine layer of moss all over these stones.

It has always been there.

But, Angus, the rest of the house is bone dry!

Aye, it is.

When does the Misty Maiden appear?

I've never seen her, mind you, but I've heard it is mainly about two o'clock in the morning.

And where in the house does she appear; that is, is there a particular room she prefers?

They say she materializes in this very room; then wanders through the rest of the house.

She starts in here?

Aye, and wherever she goes she leaves a fine misting of water on everything.

Thus the name: Misty Maiden.

Aye.

Angus, feel these stones; they are damp and cold.

They are that, lad. Perhaps the roof is leaking? No, the stones up there are quite dry.

Right, and yet, even after all these years, this huge fireplace is the only place that has moss.

T'is a bit odd, is it not.

These hearthstones seem to be set differently than the others with different mortar.

So they are.

Didn't you say they found no trace of her.

Aye.

And the commandant was an engineer, was he not?

Aye.

Angus, I wonder if she's been here all the time.

Ach, you don't think—you don't suppose—.

We stared at the floor.

Painting the Crossroad

There were two reasons why mining companies in Northern Manitoba provided summer jobs for the older teenage boys: to give them a bit of spending money; and in a subtle way, to keep them off the streets.

I was assigned to the paint crew painting pipes their identification colours; yellow for acid, blue for vacuum, and so forth.

It was an easy mindless job.

I enjoyed the new-found freedom that came with having a few dollars to spend. After contributing one-third of my cheque to the family budget, I still had quite a bit left over. Working for a living was certainly better than high school.

The new school year loomed.

So it was, at the supper table one evening, I announced that I was going to quit school and keep on working.

Mother immediately launched into a long lecture, expounding how I was too young to quit school; my whole life was ahead of me; I had to have an education; etc.

I wasn't listening.

I was waiting for Dad's reaction.

When nothing seemed forthcoming, my encouragement meter rose to new heights.

"So, you want to quit school, eh?" he intoned.

"That's for sure. I like painting much better. It's a lot easier than school."

"Um-hum," Dad agreed; at least it sounded like an

agreement. "You realize, of course, those summer jobs end when school starts."

Startled I said, "Er, no, I didn't know that."

Dad carried right on. "But, that's okay. Maybe we can find you another job."

"Great!"

Dad spread the Winnipeg Free Press across the table, and turned to the want ads.

"Let's see what you are qualified for. What skills do you have? You can paint pipes. Here, look through the listings for a pipe painter."

My scrambled search yielded nothing.

"Well, what else can you do?"

I could not think of anything.

My aspirations began to sag.

"They had you shovelling in the crushing plant for a while, didn't they? Maybe there is a need for diggers."

There wasn't.

My shoulders began to sag.

"I think there is a section for unskilled people. Have a look there."

My determined look yielded nothing. Even there, the minimum requirement was Grade Twelve.

Now it felt as if my ears were sagging.

"There is nothing here, either."

When Dad didn't offer anything more, I looked up and saw a small smile on his face. I knew I had been led down the proverbial garden path of self-realization.

I folded up the paper.

"Well, it looks like I'm going back to school."

That was the year I took my entire Grade Eleven by Manitoba Ministry of Education Correspondence, which eventually led to University and a teaching career.

Lost and Found

Just as Andrea put her hands into the dish water, the front door bell rang.

"Now what?" she muttered. "It seems as if every time I start the dishes, someone's at the door!"

She dried her hands on her apron as she strode down the hall.

She glanced at the telephone on its table and bench.

Lucy should have called by now.

The door's frosted glass showed a man's outline.

He's probably selling something.

She yanked the door open.

"Yes?" she snapped.

The tall man's immaculate three-piece suit made her think, Haven't those gone out of style?

A bland smile emanated from a face that might have been called handsome had not the features seemed deliberately designed.

"Good afternoon Ma'am. I've come to make you a special offer...."

"I don't want any," she interrupted and began closing the door.

"…to change one thing…."

As the door closed she heard, "…in your past."

With her hand still on the knob she asked her reflection in the entryway mirror, "My past?"

Andrea opened the door.

"Would you please repeat that? What did you mean: 'in my past'?"

The smile never changed.

Neither did the eyes.

"I've come to give you a chance to alter one event in your life. This is a-once-in-a-lifetime offer."

"Yeah right; it usually is."

"I have the power to grant you one wish."

Andrea leaned out and scanned the yard.

"Am I on Candid Camera?"

"No."

As Andrea peered around, the man continued.

"You can only change one incident. Can you think of anything?"

"Yeah, my husband," she said thinking how Harold left his socks lying around. She amended that perception when she considered what a good husband and father he was. "No, he's a pretty nice guy."

The stranger effused patience.

Andrea stared into ebony disinterested eyes. "You're serious aren't you?"

"Quite."

Her mind raced.

"Anything I want?"

"Yes."

"Does it have to be something big?"

"No."

"Or disastrous?"

"No."

"Life threatening?"

"No, but I cannot restore a lost life."

"Are you in a hurry? I mean, this is not something a person should rush into, make a hasty decision and all that."

Without looking at his watch the man stated, "It is now eleven-forty-three. You have five minutes."

Memories clashed: the difficult pregnancy, but she and Harold had come through it; Lucy's teenage stupidities had made life miserable, but that too was in the past; and the car accident, the whiplash, and the lawsuit were all behind her.

"I can't think of anything."

The monotone reply droned, "Three minutes."

Andrea held her hands to her cheeks. A long-suppressed desperate memory surfaced. Dare I contemplate such an aspiration? Due to society's stigma she, pregnant and unwed at seventeen, was forced to give up her baby girl.

Andrea's hand covered her quivering lips as she recalled dark hair poking out from the blanket as the nurse exited the delivery room. How often I wished I could have at least held the child, kissed her cheek, smelled her newness. What had become of her?

"Two minutes."

Her fingers stroked through her hair. Could that episode be corrected, or at least amended? Could I discover where my baby went and who had raised her? What ramifications would there be? Only Harold knew her history. What would my friends think? How would my children react? Should I take the chance?

"One minute."

"YES!" she blurted. "Could you...?"

The stranger's hand made a slow flat-circle motion between them.

"So it is requested; so it shall be done."

"But h-how? When?"

"Soon all will be revealed."

The phone rang.

"Oh, please excuse me. That is a call I've been expecting."

Andrea hurried down the hall and picked up the receiver.

She glanced back at the doorway.

The stranger was gone.

She shrugged.

"Hi Lucy, I'm glad you called."

"Er, this isn't Lucy," began a soft hesitant female voice. "You don't know me, but through an agency I've recently learned that we may be related."

Andrea had to sit down as she nearly dropped the receiver.

The Annual
Prince Charming Meeting

A cacophony of raucous voices greeted Harold as he held the meeting room door open for his master.

Prince Charming #5 addressed his servant.

"I'm sorry to drag you along to these affairs. It can't be too exciting waiting out here. I don't much like these annual Prince Charming Association meetings, but I have an important letter for the group."

"Yes sir. Might I ask why you haven't rescued a princess?"

"Let me put it this way: after seeing this lot in action, I'm not looking too hard. I shouldn't be more than an hour or two."

"Yes sir."

Harold bowed, closed the door, and then flopped into one of the ornate chairs adorning the castle hall.

I wonder what happens at my master's conferences.

Although somewhat muted, the spaces around the warped wooden door allowed Harold to discern the proceedings.

He heard three sharp raps.

"The annual meeting of the Prince Charming Association will come to order. I apologize for those who could not be here."

"They were probably not allowed to leave their castles."

"They probably had to baby-sit."

"I could come only if I promised to fix the draw bridge, which really ticks me off, because we never use the darn thing!"

"I had to sneak out. There will probably be hell to pay when I get back."

"Never mind; we all have different circumstances. The secretary will read the minutes of the last meeting."

"The meeting began at four o'clock with the minutes being adopted as read. Number 7 mentioned how dishpan hands were becoming a common complaint. Some members are suffering from arthritis in their knees, possibly brought on by scrubbing floors. Number 4 is still in the hospital after being thrown from his horse. Some members have not paid their dues. That is all."

"Are there any errors or omissions?"

"I can't pay my dues until I get my allowance."

"You get an allowance? I wish I did."

"I have to fix the castle wall before I get some more money."

"And after all the money we spent on them."

"Gentlemen, can we please get through this section? Are there any errors or omissions?"

"It was an error to take that woman to my castle."

"Right on, brother."

"HERE! HERE!"

"Gentlemen!"

"Naw, everything is there."

"Then may I have a motion to have the minutes adopted as read? - thank you; and seconder? - thank you; - all in favour? - carried. Is there any new business arising from the minutes?"

"I have a letter regarding a change in the Frog Prince's situation."

"Number 5: that will have to wait for the correspondence section. Is there any new business?"

"When is that shipment of hand cream arriving?"

"It was supposed to be here by now."

"Yeah, and will we get an increase in the hand cream allowance?"

"Number 6, you were looking into that?"

"The shipment was on its way, but was hijacked by a band of gangsters."

"Are there any leads?"

"No, other than there were seven of them, all very short, and threatened the driver with picks and shovels."

"Check with Snow White. She may have some information."

"We will leave the investigation in your capable hands, Number 6. Now if no one has any more new business, we will move to old business."

"I received a letter from the Frog Prince!"

"That is not old business. It will have to wait for the correspondence section."

"Oh, for goodness sakes, can't we just go into things?"

"Number 5, you must understand that as Prince Charmings, we must maintain a certain level of decorum, a high standard if you will. If you just wait a few minutes, we'll deal with that during correspondence."

"Oh, very well."

"Well, since there doesn't seem to be any old business, we will move to...."

"What has been happening with the Prince Charming Pension Plan?"

"You should have brought that up in the new business portion."

"I forgot."

"Ah yes, the P.C.P.P: well, I am still waiting for an answer from Castles Indemnity. Until they respond, there is not much we can do."

"I heard that the Princess' Endowment Bank has a finger in that company. You don't suppose...."

"I wouldn't put it past them, the bunch of greedy witches!"

"Gentlemen, must I remind that we rescued those damsels-in-distress, and carried them off to our castles?"

"Don't remind me."

"I'm reminded every day."

"Mine wasn't too stressed! She was sound asleep in a glass case."

"I should have let mine sleep. Now she never shuts up."

"That's nothing! I ran all over town trying to find the girl who would fit the glass slipper. I should have dropped the damn thing."

"HERE! HERE!"

Two loud raps resound.

"Gentlemen, please!"

"Yeah, and what about poor Number 9 who had the other eleven dancing princesses move in with his bride."

"And the mothers-in-law."

"Poor guy."

"His food bill must be fantastic!"

"Food is nothing. What about me? Now that Rapunzel's hair is growing back, she wants all kinds of shampoos and conditioners."

"I often wonder if I was better off when I was the beast."

"I know what you mean."

"Yeah, and how to characterize 'beast' now-a-days? No offence, Number 2."

"None taken."

"Gentlemen, let us return to the task at hand. If there's no new business, let's move to correspondence. Number 5, you had something."

"Ah yes. I heard from the Frog Prince and his situation is improving; something about a ball in a well."

"That's good to hear."

"Maybe and maybe not: personally I don't hold out much hope to get that princess to kiss him. I mean, think about it."

"Yeah, I see what you mean."

"Anyone know what she is like?"

"I heard she's cute but spoiled rotten."

"Oh-oh, that's not a good sign."

"I move that we warn him about dangers."

"I second the motion."

"There's a motion on the floor - all in favour? - carried. Number 5, will look after that? Thank you."

"When do we eat?"

"I couldn't bring very much."

"Me either."

"I ate before I came, just in case."

"Gentlemen, can we at least finish the meeting?"

"I move the meeting be adjourned."

"I'll second that!"

"All in favour?"

"AYE!"

"I'm the chair! It's the chair's responsibility to close the meeting!"

"Tell you what Number 1, since you're the chair, sit on it. The rest of us are going to eat."

"Yeah Number 1, lighten up."

"Yes, I suppose so. Okay then, I would like to propose a toast. Please raise your classes to chivalry."

"TO CHIVALRY!"

There is one rap after which only murmurings reached Harold's ears.

He dozed off.

Prince Charming
Visits a Western Saloon

A fine layer of dust covers everything except the saloon counter and the tables, where the raucous laughter of idle men fills the room.

The bar maid pastes on a smile and delivers another round to the scruffy foursome at the corner table.

She neither speaks to nor looks at them, especially the big grubby one with the shifty eyes that constantly glance around.

A horse stops somewhere outside.

Faces turn towards the swinging doors.

The impassive bar-keeper continues to wipe the latest glass.

Boots trod the wooden walkway.

The doors flap twice behind a man in an immaculate white outfit who heads for the counter.

A strange inner power emanates from him.

The bartender places a paper mat in front of the thin man. "What'll yuh have, stranger?"

The man methodically removes his long leather gloves and tucks them in his belt. "I'll have a margarita, but dispense with the rim-salt. And from the looks of things, ice is in short supply, so an extra slice of lime would be appreciated."

Snickers are heard.

The bartender ceases the glass administrations, and leans towards the gentleman. "I don't know where yer from Mister, but yuh kin have a beer or some whiskey."

"Okay then, I'll have two fingers of your best bourbon."

More snickers filter through the smoky haze.

With the patience gained through the years, the proprietor states, "Like I said, I don't know where yuh come from stranger, but 'round these parts things are pretty basic. The whiskey here is just plain spirits that come in off the eastern supply train. Now do yuh want to try again?"

"Very well then; a glass of water will be fine."

As he waits for his drink, the stranger surveys the crowd as reflected in the saloon mirror. He concludes most are brash, boisterous and basically harmless.

His interest centres upon the big guy at the corner table.

His water arrives.

"Thank you."

The bartender smiles and asks, "What brings yuh t' town. 'Pears t' me yuh are a might off track."

"I'm looking for a young lady named Snow White."

A choking splutter comes from the corner table.

Regaining control and wiping his face, the large man asks, "Who wants to know?"

The stranger slowly turns, rests his elbows on the counter, and says, "I do."

"And who might you be?"

"The guy who wants to know."

"A wise guy eh? What are you called?"

"I'm known as Pee Cee."

"What kinda name is that?"

"There is a reason. What is your appellation?"

"My what?"

"Your name? Your handle?"

"I'm Harvey, foreman of the Queen Ranch."

"Like I said, I am making inquiries about a certain young lady whom, I understand, was kidnapped by a person or persons unknown."

"Well, yuh won't gitno information from anyone around here, will he?"

Customers stare at their drinks.

"My preliminary investigations indicate that the Queen Ranch is involved with her disappearance. I'm sure someone here knows what happened."

With a growl, the large scruffy man confronts the stranger. His finger jabs the white vest. "Look, we don't need the likes of you snooping around our little town."

"I very much doubt if that is the unanimous opinion of the present company. Maybe I should start my enquiries with you."

The dirty finger continues to poke. "Stranger, I suggest you git back on your horse and don't come back."

The stranger smiles.

The eyes do not.

A dead-calm voice says, "I suggest that you stop with the finger."

"Or you'll stop me?"

"Yes."

"You and whose army?"

The thin man jabs a finger into the bully's shoulder.

A howl of pain is followed by, "I can't move my arm!"

"It will return to normal about this time tomorrow," says the man-in-white. "Now I understand you know something about her disappearance."

Defiant hate oozes from Harvey. "I'm not telling yuhnuthin'."

"Would you like the other arm to match?"

Reality registers in wide pain-filled eyes.

Bruiser shakes his head.

"Now, tell me about Snow White's sudden departure."

Bruiser struggles with the confession.

"My boss's wife told me to take her out into the desert and leave her there."

"And?"

"She was so pretty and all; I couldn't leave her there. I gave her to a group of miners that were heading for their claim. They were looking for a cook and housekeeper. That's all I know."

"Thank you. At least I know you have some feelings. Now can you tell me where their mining camp might be?"

Bruiser nods. "S'far as I know - never been there - but I think its t'wards the upper end of Paradise River, about a two or three day ride north of here."

"Thank you very much. See, that wasn't too difficult, was it?"

The stranger finishes his water.

"If I am to visit those miners, I'd better get going while there is still some daylight."

The bartender leans towards him.

"I'd like t' offer a bit of advice. Folks don't cotton t' things they don't understand. A name like Pee Cee could lead to problems."

"I'm not too worried." The man glances at Bruiser. "Things can usually be resolved."

The bartender shrugs. "Okay. By the way, what does the Pee Cee stand for?"

"Prince Charming."

The doors flap twice.

Jack and the Beanstalk

The judge rapped his gavel.

"Next case."

As a file was handed to the judge, a lawyer ushered in a worried lady and a teenage boy into the courtroom.

In a commanding voice the clerk announced, "The Fantasy World vs Jack on the charge of murder, robbery and community endangerment."

The lawyer stood up. "My client pleads 'not guilty'."

The judge scowled at the file and then at the clerk. "What the hell is this: a murder accusation in a fairy tale? Who initiated this charge?"

"The wife of the dead Ogre did, because she has been left bereft and alone in the clouds."

The judge shook his head. "This isn't happening."

Then Jack's lawyer stood up. "It is a clear case of self-defence, your honour."

The judge took a deep breath. "Well, what are the facts?"

The clerk continued. "A couple of days ago the accused cut down a beanstalk and an Ogre was killed."

"There are still Ogres around?"

"One less, your honour, but this particular Ogre had stolen this family's money and killed the father."

"Why wasn't it reported?"

"It was sir, but the Ogre escaped to his castle in the sky. It was only recently made possible to reach the clouds due to a bean stalk that grew from some beans Jack traded for his mom's cow."

The judge frowned at Jack. "You traded a perfectly good cow for some beans?"

"Er, yes sir, but the man said they were magic beans."

"What did your Mom say when you got home?"

"She was very angry. She threw them out the window and sent me to bed with no supper."

"You got off lucky."

Jack became animated. "Yeah, but over night, a huge beanstalk grew up. Its top was in the clouds where the Ogre lived. I told Mom I would climb up and take our money back. So I did."

"So," the judge said, "This is where larceny was added to the charges."

"I don't know nuthin about no larceny sir, but I took back the money what was ours. It was all mixed in with the Ogre's money so I took the whole bag. I heard him bragging how the bag kept refilling itself."

Jack smiled at his Mom.

"I went to grab the magic harp too, but the stupid thing woke up the Ogre when it yelled, Master! Master!"

The lawyer started, "Your honour..."

The judge held up a hand. "Let the boy talk."

"That's when the Ogre started chasing me."

"I'm not surprised."

"I was faster climbing down the bean stalk because the Ogre

found it slippery. I yelled to Mom to get the axe. As soon as I hit the ground I started chopping. And down crashed the big stalk with the Ogre on it."

The clerk whispered to the judge.

"I have just been informed that the vine crushed some houses on the street and injured several neighbours."

The lawyer stood. "The collateral damage was unintended, sir."

The judge leaned back into his chair and put his fingers together.

After a few minutes he leafed through some old tattered books and studied specific pages.

The room became quiet while he made some notes.

Finally he leaned forward.

"The court has come to a decision. From the past cases such as Snow White and Hansel and Gretel, the demise of the witches was justified. No charges were laid. So it shall be with the death of the Ogre. Concerning the neighbourhood disruption, the recovered money will be used to rebuild the damaged homes and also pay for medical expenses. That is all."

The lawyer bowed. "Thank you, your honour."

The gavel crashed once.

"Next case!"

The Un-Princed Frog

"Enough is enough! That damn frog has kept me awake all night!"

I threw back the covers, slammed on my hat, grabbed my magic wand, and stomped to the open window.

Silhouetted in the reflection of the full moon sat the amplified amphibian on his lily pad stage.

I shook my wand at it. "Give me a break!" I yelled. "If you don't keep quiet, I'll turn you into a prince!"

Concentric waves radiated from the frog's position.

"Oh, Miss Witch," it begged, "Please don't do that. It would be a fate worse than death!"

Surprised, I asked why.

The frog relaxed. "Well, think about it. I'd have to scramble through thorny forests; climb high mountains; battle inclement weather; and fight fiery dragons; all in an effort to rescue some damsel in distress. After taking her to my castle, she would probably whine all day about the décor and cry all night from missing her dad. Her nagging would drive me crazy!"

I laughed.

"Tell you what," it continued. "Let's compromise. I'll serenade the ladies in the evenings and be quiet late at night."

"Sounds like a plan. Good night, frog."

"Good night, witch."

I slept soundly.

An Alpine Appetizer

Once upon a time high in the Alps, Gorton, the troll who guarded the south bridge, decided to visit his compadre in charge of the north crossover.

"That Orton guy is always looking for an easy meal."

Gorton gave the large stew pot a final stir and then slid it towards the back of the stove.

After some hard up-hill slogging his stubby legs brought him to a puffing halt at a stone wall behind which his friend was slaving in a recently created garden.

"Hey Orton, where have you been?" he asked the haggard troll.

The gaunt elf stood up and rubbed his back.

"Oh, I've taken up gardening. It's a lot safer than guarding that north bridge. Want a carrot?"

"No thanks. I can't stay long. I have to keep my eye on my stew back home. But I have to ask: What happened to you? You look terrible. You were one of the most feared trolls in these mountains."

Orton grimaced. "Actually, it's my own fault when I tried to make a major score."

"And?"

Gorton's friend scuffed the dirt. "I'm almost embarrassed to talk about it."

"I promise I won't laugh."

"You know those three Gruff Goats that romped up on the north side there?"

"Yeah."

Orton paused and scratched his head. "Come to think of it, I've only seen two lately."

"Never mind that," Gorton urged. "Go on with your story."

"Well anyway, one day they decided to cross my bridge, probably to get at that fresh grass on the east side. When I stopped the little one, he begged for me to wait for a bigger friend that would be coming."

"And did you?"

"Yup, and along came this fat female. I was about to put her in the freezer when her big sad eyes persuaded me to wait for an even bigger one!"

Gorton sagged. "You didn't?"

"Yeah," Orton sighed. "When I stepped in front of the big one, he charged and butted me into the river! It was weeks before I could breathe without pain." Orton winced, "It still hurts to talk about it."

"You poor chap, you'd better come on to my house. A rest will do you good."

"Okay. I'll bring some beans, peas, and carrots. Want to grab that basket of potatoes?"

After an enjoyable stroll, the two entered a humble hut under a stone bridge.

"Well, here we are," announced Gorton. "Please excuse the mess. It was quite exciting here a little while ago."

"I'm glad someone is having some fun. Whatever you're cooking certainly smells delicious. What is in the pot?"

Gorton grinned. "You've heard the saying: A bird in the hand...?"

"...Is worth two in the bush. Yeah, I know that one."

"Well, that is Baby Goat Gruff. Want a leg?"

Small but Important

Once upon a time the minerals held a conference call to decide the location for their annual Colour Convention.

"Where should we go this time?" said Ruby.

"Yeah," said Amethyst, "We are all so pretty, we can't just meet anywhere."

"Well," pondered the Pink Tourmaline, "Since we've been all over the world, why not meet at a secluded place where we can still show off our colours."

"Let's meet at Old Remnant's place," said Emerald. It is nice and sunny where he is."

The Black Onyx sneered. "We can bug Beige at the same time. He certainly isn't going to go anywhere, not with Old Remnant sitting on him."

A chorus rang out: "Sounds great; see you there."

Old Remnant was a huge boulder that had been deposited by the last retreating glacier. It had been left resting high upon a smooth Precambrian rock face that slanted steeply towards a deep lake.

The only thing preventing the gigantic rock from tumbling into the lake was a small beige stone wedged under it.

"Hi Beige," said White Quartzite. "We've come to have our yearly meeting with you and Remnant."

"And to needle me just because we stones are not as pretty as you guys. I know what Onyx thinks of us.

"Sorry," said Onyx, "I was just teasing."

"Never mind all that," said Old Remnant. "I'm glad you're here. What have you and your relatives been doing?"

Blue Sapphire stated, "One of my close relatives is decorating a princess's hand."

"Yeah," said Yellow Sapphire, "My clear yellow crystals are becoming very popular."

"A new raja has a relative of mine in his crown," said Ruby.

Emerald strutted. "In Colombia, people are constantly fighting over me and my kin."

Carnelian whined, "I wish more humans knew about my lovely orange colour."

Amethyst spoke up. "I may not be as precious as Ruby there. My purple crystalline structure makes me very difficult to polish into jewellery."

"That is just like me," said Tourmaline. My deep pink makes lovely brooches and rings."

With the news exhausted and a lull in the conversation, the arrogant group turned its attention to Beige, the stone.

Quartzite said, "I'm sorry if we appear to brag a bit. We gems and semi-precious stones don't know what it is like to be just a...."

"Just a rock," finished Beige. "We stones may not be as glamorous as you lot, but some of us have hidden talents and important jobs."

At the front of Remnant, the gems gathered around Onyx as it challenged, "And what do you have that is so valuable?"

"Yeah," said Ruby, "Show us what you have."

The rest took up the refrain: "Show us! Show us!"

"I can't," said Beige. "I am nothing. I have nothing!"

"Maybe I can help," Remnant boomed, and pressed down on Beige.

"Don't! Don't" Beige yelled.

"Do it! Do it!" The gang cheered.

Suddenly Beige shattered.

Old Remnant teetered, toppled, and then propelled the mineral group into the lake.

Huge waves washed up on the shore.

As silence returned to the Canadian Shield, Beige looked at his broken sections.

"I tried to tell them that sometime little people have important jobs."

Another Time –
Same Place

The author relaxed and then opened a long-neglected unfinished story.

Hi.

Hi.

I'm glad you're back.

Yes, finally.

I've missed you.

I missed you too.

It's been a long time.

Too long.

Where did you go?

I've been busy.

Oh sure; probably with other characters.

There were priorities; deadlines, contests, the like.

You know I can't live without you!

Yes but...

Even time has no meaning.

I understand that but...

I come alive when you are around.

I know, but so do many others.

You introduced me to that mysterious gentleman who was, shall we say, interested.

I remember.

And that intimate dining experience was extraordinary.

The Moroccan Kasbah Restaurant; I thought you'd like that.

I'm still wearing that low-cut black gown and the pearls.

Good.

My hair is perfect.

You look great.

And Henry was saying all the right things and giving signals.

Anticipation is half the fun.

Yes! But just as things were warming up, you left!

I had a contest deadline.

What about MY deadline? I'm looking forward to getting – well - you know....

Exactly; well, let's see what I can do.

The author began writing.

The Writer
Is Blocked, er Bombed

The collection of empties was growing.

To escape the cursor's incessant blinking I had retreated to my lumpy sofa where I could ponder the multitude of mental images and ideas, none of which had any coherent connection.

This wasn't the first time.

It was during these non-creative times that my invisible friend, Beverly, materialized on the end of the couch.

I hated her, her and her arrogant attitude haranguing me about my procrastinations.

"Wha' the hell - hic - what th' hell do you know, eh?" I yelled so she would hear me good, or well, or better, or whatever. "I can write something any time I want, ya know. It's just that there's no time, and even if there was time, I hafta to catch up on other things, which means there'd be no time for me to write what you want me to write, so then the other stuff would get behind and...."

I stopped. If she wasn't satisfied with that bit of logic, then one of us didn't know what we were talking about.

She grinned as she hovered above the armrest.

Her silence was deafening.

I wasn't about to let her get away with that. I'd fix her, her and that supercilious smirk.

I squinted real hard so that I could see better, and waggled a finger or two at her.

"Yuh know, if you'd quit moving, I could talk better. Now you wait right there while I get another brew, and then we'll straighten this out once and f'rall."

She levitated higher as I rolled off the couch.

When I woke up Beverly was gone. She probably didn't want to lose another argument. Maybe her head was pounding as much as mine.

A groan escaped when I saw the cursor patiently waiting for inspiration and blinking on, off, on, off, on....

Maxwell Moose

Maxwell Moose had always lived in the boreal forest where the air was fresh and food and clean water was plentiful.

Every day he met other residents such as squirrels, chipmunks, foxes, and porcupines, and various birds ranging from Chickadees to Great Horned Owls.

He particularly liked the late spring when new family members played around his white-stocking legs.

At the pond, while munching on his favourite food, lily pad roots, he watched beavers at work, while mink and otters prowled the shoreline where herons and bitterns hunted. Often his cousin, the White Tailed Deer, came by to drink.

Lately Max began meeting many new residents.

"Where did all of you come from?" he asked them. "What happened to your homes?"

Some answers he received were: "They're all gone." "Destroyed." "Torn up." "Cut down." "There is nothing left!"

Max thought, 'If humans were doing anything in the bush the Canada Jay – nicknamed Whiskey Jack - would know about it since he hangs around human campsites.'

He asked Raven to let Whiskey know that Max would like to see him.

As Maxwell waited, he studied the forest. Although the trees appeared to be the same, to a trained eye like his, the wide range of maturity levels soon became apparent.

The majestic mature trees shaded the immature ones which in turn sheltered the seedlings growing in the moss.

All was in harmony.

"What's up?" Whiskey asked as he landed on Max's brown back.

"Whiskey, you always look so trim in your grey tuxedo."

"Thank you; I do like to be neat. Raven said you wanted to see me."

"Yes," said Max. "There are a lot of new faces in this section of forest. They said their homes were destroyed. Are humans operating in the bush again?"

"Yes," said Whiskey. "They are logging on the other side of the second hill."

"My grandson is over there! Let's go have a look and see how he is doing."

As Max strode over the rough terrain, he recalled what his grandparents had taught him about humans logging.

"We did not worry about the humans in the bush," his grandpa had said. "When they cut down the mature trees, horses pulled the logs out from between the younger trees. It was a good system. The younger trees continued to grow and the seedlings were not unduly disturbed.

"After the wood cutters left, there was space for us to nibble on the tall bushes and new plants that filled in the holes. It was great."

As Max edged around another muskeg area, he found his grandson crying in a thick clump of alders.

"Grandson, what is the matter? Why aren't you at home?"

Upon seeing his grandpa, the grandson ran over. "Oh Grandpa, it's terrible. I have no home. There is nothing left!"

"Oh Grandson, it can't be that bad."

"Yes it is, Grandpa, you'll see!"

"Well, lead the way."

As the threesome cleared the top of the second hill, Grandpa blinked.

A wasteland of jumbled branches, crushed uprooted trees, and torn terrain confronted him. A few scraggly poplars and birches baked in the sun.

Max could hardly speak.

"See what I mean, Grandpa."

"This is where humans are logging," Whiskey said.

"This isn't logging! This is devastation!"

"It's called clear cutting," said Whiskey. "It is a logging practice which involves completely clearing an area of trees, regardless of their size and usability.

"I don't care what it is called; it's disgraceful!"

"Pretty stupid, eh?" said Whiskey. "Companies do it because it is more efficient; at least that is the excuse they use."

"Aren't there laws that prevent this?"

Whiskey nodded his head. "Yes, but humans are very hard to understand. The natural resource laws they design favour the lumber companies."

The moss crunched and cracked on the desiccated ground as Max strolled through the rubble. Wrinkled blueberries drooped from shrivelled bushes. He prodded limp seedlings.

"This is terrible," Max growled. "Don't they realize that the abrupt removal of trees can have a serious environmental impact?

"A forest traps and retains rain water. Without tree-cover the water runs away rather than filtering into the water table. A fast runoff can cause flooding, and take valuable topsoil with it."

Max looked at the dying poplar trees in the barren landscape. "Now I know why there were so many new-comers to my area."

Grandpa Max stomped his foot.

"Look at this!" Max snapped. "They've cleared right up to the river!"

"What is wrong with that, Grandpa?"

"Grandson, if a river loses its shade, the water temperature rises. A change of a few degrees makes a huge impact to native plants, fish, and amphibians,"

Whiskey shook his head. "The law says the company must leave a forested strip along the banks. As I cruise the forest, I notice that the logging companies purposely leave a strip of forest on either side of the highways so that travellers can't see the clear cut areas."

"This is worse than a forest fire," said Max, as he recalled his mother's conversation about wild fires.

"Max," she had said, "Although it is true that fires are destructive, they do not destroy everything.

"Sometimes the flames dance across the tree-tops but leave the ground cover unharmed. Occasionally the fire will creep along the ground, and the tree tops go untouched. At times a fire will leave large patches of bush undamaged.

"After the fire is out, pine cones open and shed their seeds. A carpet of purple fireweed grows as if attempting to cover the destruction. Seedlings of poplar, birch and alders soon sprout and, together with grasses, bind the soil. It takes a while but the area does recover."

Grandson Moose stared at the desolation. "Can this be fixed?"

Whiskey spoke up. "I've been around humans, and I have learned that they can also be resourceful. The government does reforestation. The Ministry of Natural Resources has nurseries where it grows thousands of seedlings that are planted in cut-over areas."

"That's good," said Grandson Moose, "But it will be decades before the trees, if they survive, can be harvested."

"And the number of trees planted is far less than the amount removed," added Whiskey.

"At that rate," observed Max, "In a few years there won't be any usable trees."

"What am I going to do, Grandpa?"

"There is not much we can do, Grandson. You will have to come and live in my territory for now."

"Well, if you don't need me any more," said Whiskey, "I think I'll fly over to the lake where some fishermen are camping. They usually have a few scraps to spare. Take care, you two."

"Goodbye Whiskey, said Max. "Thank you for all your help."

As Whiskey disappeared, Grandpa Max said, "Come on Grandson; let's go home…while we still have one."

As the two plodded onward, his grandson's voice broke through Max's thoughts.

"I did not realize humans were so destructive."

"Grandson, all animals believe, that during the formation of the planet, the one thing the earth did not need was mankind."

A Camping Staple

The cool drizzly day delayed further activities.

Miserable and cold, with bowls and spoons in hand, we huddled around the upwind side of the campfire, and gratefully absorbed its radiated warmth.

Above the pile of shimmering coals, a blackened pot's lid predicted a warmer future as periodic puffs of steam escaped.

Lipton's Chicken Noodle Soup was coming.

When the yellow translucent liquid, with its three-quarter-inch noodles, was finally ladled out, each camper cuddled the bowl, and allowed that mind-etching aroma to envelope the nasal passages.

Personal thoughts internalized, perhaps imagining how great it would be – at this precise moment - to soak one's feet in a warm broth-bath.

Like miniature sail boats dotting an amber sea, parsley flecks spun and flowed on invisible currents spawned by the cooling mixture.

Rebelling against the heat, and blowing over each spoonful, tongues and lips savoured the salty 'chicken' bisque.

A heartfelt: "Man, this sure hits the spot," was echoed by the nods or murmurs of others.

All too soon spoons were scraping plastic bowls.

After a paper towel was used to wipe out the dish, the renewed focus was on the blue enamel coffee pot hanging from the fire hook. Hot brew delivered into plastic mugs provided both external and internal warmth.

Satisfied sighs followed each sip.

Creaking trees, rustling branches, and snapping cedar branches in the fire interrupted the silence.

A loon's melancholy moan faded down the lake.

Friends scanned the western skyline.

Someone commented, "I certainly hope it's a better day tomorrow."

The Auction Advertisement

Nine-year old Jeremy and his eleven-year-old sister flopped at opposite ends of the couch, and stared at the blank television screen.

"I'm going to miss Grandma," Angela sighed. "I didn't think I would but...." Her voice trailed off.

"Yeah, me too," Jeremy added, "even though she was cranky."

"I sure didn't want to go to her funeral," Angela gritted, "seeing her lying there and all."

"Yeah, it was awful."

They became lost in their own thoughts.

Angela broke in. "I suppose we'll have to go the auction with mom and dad. I'd rather stay home."

"Me too. Mom and dad have been in and out of Grandma's house all week."

Angela went to the dining room table. "Mom left the newspaper here," Angela said as she spread out the sheets.

They soon located the auction write-up.

"What does it say?" asked Jeremy.

"It talks about a Victorian oval dining table. It's probably the one we all sat around at Christmas time."

"Yeah I remember. The chairs were too big for me. What else?"

Angela pointed. "Hm, well there is a grandfather clock."

"Oh, that stupid thing! Grandma was real mad when I pulled up the weights that were way down. I wasn't going to break it!"

His sister smiled. "I know that, but she didn't. It says there are piano stools. I hated those things and the piano lessons."

"Yeah, remember how she always said, 'Music is good for you.'"

The two continued to scan the ad.

"What's a spinet desk?" Jeremy asked. "Did grandma sew on it?"

"I don't think so. It's that table that was up in her study. It's a desk where half the top flops back onto the other half and you can put stuff inside."

"Oh yeah, I remember looking inside it one day when she came in. "'That's none of your affair.'" Jeremy mimicked.

Angela stared at her brother. "You knew she was very particular about her stuff."

"Yeah, I know, but every time we went for a visit, I felt as if I had to keep my hands in my pockets."

Angela read some more. "Moser Crystal, Royal Worchester dessert service, large selection of class and china, Doulton Figures...."

Jeremy burst in. "Doulton Figures! That's those stupid china dolls she had everywhere. She never did anything with them. All they did was gather dust."

"They weren't toys, Jeremy! Some are worth hundreds of dollars."

"Well, it was a waste of money as far as I can see. I wasn't even allowed to pick one up to look at it."

"Don't feel bad; neither was I."

The children sat back in the chairs.

"Oh well," sighed Angela, "at least I have that patch-work quilt she made for my bed."

"She made one for me, too."

"It must have been a lot of work for her."

They stared at the ad.

"I'm going to miss Grandma," Angela stated.

"Me too," said Jeremy. "At least she will be with us in the quilts."

"True," added his sister. "We could say we have her love to keep us warm."

Grannie's Sky

The name Dr. Henry Laird shone in my headlights as I parked in my designated slot in the observatory's parking lot.

I stepped out into one of those gorgeous velvet-black penetrating nights that make the telescope's task so much easier.

Looking up I glanced at Orion's sword and the nebula M42. As part of a research paper, I planned to compare the changes in The Trapezium from data documented fifty years ago.

As I stood looking at the innumerable stars and galaxies, a meteor slashed the sky.

It was a Grannie Sky.

I thought of Grandma.

It was on a night such as this - one of those clear warm prairie nights – that I had climbed the hill on Grandma's farm where I had spent the summer.

I instantly recalled the entire experience.

After a dismal Grade Eleven, Dad 'suggested' I go and give Grandma a hand on her small isolated farm in Saskatchewan.

After the long bus ride to Estevan which dropped me off at the end of Drapo Lane – shortened from Drapozyvitz Lane - by the local bus line, I was positive the whole idea was a big mistake.

Grandma must have been watching for me, for I no sooner

started down her road when she — wiping her hands on her apron - hustled out the front door.

When I noticed she was limping, I jogged so that she would not have to walk as far.

Grandma smelled of fresh homemade bread when we hugged.

"Oh, it's so good to see you, Henry," she said in the wonderful Ukrainian lilt I had grown to love. "My how you've grown!"

"Good to see you too, Grannie," I smiled.

"Come in. Come in. You must be tired. I vill show you to your room and then we vill have some fresh bread with homemade strawberry jam."

About a third of a loaf remained by the time I put down my knife. Life was taking on a whole new perspective.

Although it was a tiny farm, there always seemed to be lots to do. She had already planted the garden, so I helped with the weeding after I learned how to tell a weed from a new plant.

Since there wasn't much else to do — trying to watch her snowy television was a real pain — I soon learned to do things without being asked.

She put me in charge of the chickens while she looked after the two cows. When we cleaned the stalls, I forked out the spoiled straw while she spread the fresh bedding.

In the evening, after the chores were done, we'd build a small bonfire. I'd roast marshmallows while she knitted - it was amazing how she could knit with just the light from the fire - often staying up long after we — especially Grannie - should have gone to bed.

I knew Mom had spoken with her. I kept waiting for Grannie to ask a bunch of dumb questions such as: How is school going? Why didn't I study harder? What was I planning to do with my life? But she never did! Somehow I wound up doing most of the talking.

Even while working alone, I would hear Grannie's voice in the background.

"Life does not happen all at once. It is like a chain of interconnected segments. You must make each link strong because you do not know its relationship to the others until much later in life."

With the new school year approaching, I was not looking forward to returning to the city. Even with all the hard work, it was going to be really

difficult leaving Grannie.

It was on one of those last nights that I, feeling somewhat edgy, was using a burning twig to make fiery drawings in the air.

Suddenly she plopped her knitting into her lap.

"Henry," she scowled, "Did you know that people are like different types of wood. Some people are like that dry stick you're waving around. They flare brightly but don't leave much of a mark. Others are like those pieces of maple in the fire there. It takes a long time for them to get going, but once they start, the impression they leave upon society is felt for a long time, sometimes forever."

I stopped.

"What kind of wood am I, Grannie?"

She continued clicking her needles.

Finally she stopped and looked right at me.

"Well, Henry," she began, "Let me put it this way: you are certainly a much better quality wood now than when you first arrived, if you know what I mean."

She resumed her knitting.

"I think so," I said, but deep down inside I knew exactly what she meant.

"Er, Grannie, would you mind very much if I went for a walk, just up the hill there?"

She looked up. "Of course not, but mind you walk slowly so you don't sprain your ankle."

"I'll be careful, Grannie," I laughed and went to put a few small logs on the coals.

"Oh, don't worry about the fire. I'll be going inside in a few minutes anyway."

I gave her a quick hug and headed for the hill.

And so it was, with her latest piece of philosophy playing in my head, I found a soft indentation in the hill, lay down, and stared up at the stars.

The only part I liked about last year's science class was astronomy and the excitement I felt when learning about millions of galaxies like ours.

I soon located Cassiopeia and Orion with its belt. The Big Dipper was next, and it pointed to the Polaris at the end of the Little Dipper's handle. I finally found the Drago wrapped around the Little Dipper.

When I remembered the right toe was the white giant star Rigel, I looked back at Polaris and thought, 'You would think that an important star like Polaris would be brighter.'

Grannie's gentle words filtered in: "Sometimes a small

contribution to mankind lasts longer than some exciting knick-knack that benefits very few."

A meteor sliced the speckled inkiness.

Again Grannie's words flashed across my mind: "Some people have a momentary blaze of glory and then vanish."

As I headed down that hill, I resolved to become an astronomer, and perhaps become a 'star' in my Grannie's heaven.

A low rumble overhead indicated the telescope doors were opening in preparation for tonight's exploration.

A tear trembled on my cheek.

I waved at the star-studded sky - at my Grannie's Sky.

"Good night, Grandma."

Hanging Out with Mona Lisa

It was Saturday. Harry and James stood on the bank and flicked stones into the river.

"I hate weekends," grumped James. "As much as I hate Grade5, at least there is something to do in school."

"Yeah, we can play baseball or soccer with the gang. I never see anyone on the weekends."

James glanced at the art gallery across the street. "Wanna go look at some pictures?"

"Sure."

After they had wandered around for a while, Harry approached a gallery employee.

"That painting of the Mona Lisa must be a copy otherwise you guys would have a guard on it, right?"

The man smiled. "That's correct, young man. That is an excellent forgery our gallery obtained. The details are all there."

"Thank you, sir," said Harry. "Come on James, let's have a good look."

The boys stood apart as they studied the Mona Lisa painting.

"She's staring at me," James stated.

"No, she is looking at me."

James huffed. "She can't look at both of us at the same time, otherwise her eyes would cross or move or something."

"Well, let's see." Harry moved such that he passed behind his younger brother and on over to the other side. "See! She watched me all the time."

"Her eyes never moved!"

"Hm, there must be something about the eyes of people in pictures that we don't understand."

"Do you think she's pretty?"

"Nope, especially not with all that stringy hair," Harry pointed. "It looks like she just washed it."

"Jessica looks like that when she comes out of the bathroom."

They laughed as they pictured their sister.

"Is she smiling?" asked James.

"It's hard to tell. Maybe she was told to smile but didn't want to show her broken tooth."

They chortled again.

Harry bent closer. "Look at her hands. I don't think she does any hard work. There is no dirt on them."

"She probably has servants to do the washing and cooking while she sits around. Those aren't poor-people clothes."

"I wonder if she lives in a castle."

"I don't know. It's hard to tell, but there is a weird red road way down below."

"Hey, James, look at that scenery behind her. Does it remind you of something?"

"Yeah! It's just like our Crossed Swords computer game. Let's go and play it."

"Good idea. We haven't played it for a while."

James and Harry hurried home.

The Wallet

For Jeremy it was another boring small-town summer-holiday's day. He certainly would be glad when school started when he'd have a new teacher for his Grade 5-6 class.

His Mom was watching her programs, so he grabbed a banana and headed outside.

Up town he strolled along the main street where the bank, hotel and general store faced the town hall, police station, and post office.

At the park's fountain, he passed the old man who was sitting there. Jeremy's Mom had told him never to bother the sad. elderly man from Mrs. Olson's rooming house.

At the edge of town Jeremy stopped at the burned house that was overgrown with small trees and bushes. It had been there as long as he could remember. A section of a white picket fence poked through the tall grass.

Someone said a mother and her two children had died there while the father was away at a war.

Jeremy rolled his favourite marble — the clear green one - between his fingers. As he held it up to his eye, he tripped and watched the glass ball disappear into a pile of blackened boards.

He scowled as he searched, because every time he moved something, the marble rolled deeper. Jeremy persisted until he found it resting beside something wrapped up in oilcloth. It was a wallet! Somehow the checked fabric had preserved it.

A quick search yielded a few coins in the pouch, some photos, and a strange key stuck in the back corner.

He flipped through the black and white photos: A lady, all dressed up, was standing in front of a small house with a white fence; the same lady holding a baby; the same woman standing with a girl and a boy; a horse and milk wagon; a soldier at the train station; and an old driver's licence where the smeared name looked like Jenson or Jemson.

I'll show Mom; maybe she can tell me about the pictures.

After using some sand and rainwater to clean his hands, he headed home.

As he passed the old man, Jeremy blurted, "Wanna see what I found?"

Tired sad eyes looked up. "Sure," the man answered in a distinctly disinterested tone.

"See? It's a wallet. I found it in that old burned house over there. There are some neat pictures in it."

The man straightened and extended a weathered hand. "May I please look at it?"

"Sure," said Jeremy handing over the wallet and then sitting on the bench.

The gentleman turned to the pictures. Old fingers caressed each photo.

"Do you know any of those people?"

"Yes," the man nodded. "This was a billfold I had long time ago. This is - was - my family."

"Was?" Jeremy blurted, and then instinctively put his hand on his mouth. "You mean...?"

The old man nodded and continued to flick through the images.

Unsure of what to do Jeremy looked at his hands.

"That burned house was yours, wasn't it?"

"Yes," acknowledged a soft whisper.

"Mom told me something about the fire; that somebody had died there a long time ago."

Jeremy heard a whimper and a moan, and then the man buried his face in his hands.

The billfold dangled from his fingers.

Jeremy glanced at the shaking shoulders. Should he leave? Something told him to stay put, so he fiddled with his marble.

After a few minutes the man sat back and sighed.

"Sorry, mister," muttered Jeremy, "I didn't mean to upset you."

"No need to be, son." A smile fluttered as the man dabbed his eyes with a ratty tissue. "It's a deep hurt that goes away back, long before your time. A cry is always good for the soul." He looked at Jeremy. "What's your name, young man?"

"Jeremy Hansen."

"I'm Bill Jensen."

They shook hands.

"Would you like me to tell you about the pictures?"

"Yes, please."

Wrinkled fingers lovingly stroked the first picture. "This is – was – my Jenny. She worked in the malt shop at the milk company I worked for." The man leaned towards Jeremy. "She made the best chocolate milk shakes. After my deliveries, I would buy one and take my time drinking it."

"'Cause you wanted to be close to her, right?"

"That's right." Bright eyes shone with memories. "Eventually I asked her out. We went for walks and picnics and the Saturday night dances."

"And watched TV," anticipated Jeremy.

The old gentleman laughed. "There was no television back then. You made your own entertainment."

"That must have been a long time ago."

"It must seem like that to you." The man relaxed. "Well, when the owner became ill, he asked if I would like to buy the company. So I did."

"Then Jenny worked for you."

"Yes, but I soon hired someone do the malt shop, while she looked after the account books. She always found ways to tighten loose ends and do things better. She was really great."

The man smiled with recollections.

"Did you quit the deliveries?" asked Jeremy.

"Not right away. I liked the outdoors, so I stayed with it for a while."

The man flipped a few photos. "This is my horse and wagon. That horse knew the route better than I did. I could jump off with my rack of bottles and he would keep going and stop at the place where I needed a refill."

"Smart horse."

"Yup, he sure was." He leaned towards Jeremy. "Well, you know, since I had a bit more money, I asked Jenny to marry me."

"I'm glad."

"Me too. We got married and moved into a little house with a white picket fence."

The man flipped to the beginning of the pictures. "You can see it behind her in this picture. It was a good place for raising a family. There was lots of room and a garden out the back. We had many happy years there; raised two kids: a girl first and then a boy."

The man flipped the photos. "This is Gloria and Ryan standing with Jenny."

"Ryan looks about my age."

"He is about nine years old in that photo. But then the war started. I, and a lot of friends, joined up and went overseas. That's me, Private Jenson, at the train station."

The man paused and stroked the photo. "I was away for about two years when the fire...."

The man covered his mouth with the back of his hand.

After a few moments he continued. "The army sent me home, but by the time I got here, everything had been done. The town had had a funeral with three closed caskets. The markers were donated."

The voice struggled. "Apparently there wasn't much to...to bury."

Again the man buried his face in his hands.

Jeremy patted the shaking shoulders. It seemed the right thing to do.

Finally the man sat back, wiped his eyes and stared at the wallet. "I apologize for acting like this. I did not mean to bother you with my troubles."

"I don't mind."

The old gentleman made a little chuckle. He took in a deep breath, held it and slowly exhaled. "What strange twist of fate. You have helped me deal with a nagging piece of my life. Thank you, Jeremy."

The boy shrugged. "I just found your wallet. Did you see the key in there?"

The man fingered the key. "This looks like a safety-deposit box key. I remember having one long time ago." He looked at Jeremy. "You don't suppose there is something still in there? That's still the same bank. I suppose it wouldn't hurt to ask, eh?"

The man stood up. "Here is your wallet."

"Oh no, it's your wallet. You keep it. I'm glad you found it."

Jeremy relaxed on the bench and watched the man enter the bank.

Jeremy polished his marble on his shirt and tried to peer through it. When he looked up, he saw Mr. Jensen beckoning him.

Jeremy ran over. "Did you find some money?"

Mr. Jensen clutched some papers against his chest. There were tears in his eyes, and yet he seemed happy.

He held out a packet of papers. "These are far more valuable than money. These are our wedding pictures, our marriage licence, and photos of when the kids were first born. Even their baptism certificates are here! Thanks to you, I have a piece of my life – my past – to hold onto."

They stood looking at the papers.

Jeremy broke the silence. "Well, sir, I'd better be going. Mom will have supper ready. Goodbye, Mr. Jensen."

"Goodbye, Jeremy. I'm glad we met."

"Me too."

They shook hands.

Jeremy ran home where, as he burst into the kitchen, he called out, "Hey Mom, I was over at that burned-down house, and I found a wallet and guess what?"

Pocketing Pieces
of the Day

"And change those shorts before you go out," his mom called from the kitchen. "They're filthy."

Terry pursed his lips and nodded.

"I don't know how you can wear the same clothes day in and day out."

"'Cause they're comfortable," he mumbled at the mirror.

"And clean out the pockets before you put them in the wash."

"Yeah, yeah."

"I don't want to find a pile like I did last time. Heaven knows why you keep such stuff."

"It's not stuff."

"Every time I do the wash I have to go through your pockets."

Terry grimaced. He'd heard it all before.

"I have better things to do…"

He quietly closed the door, and turned on his radio.

He donned the blue shorts, picked up his favourite tan ones, and then emptied its pockets onto the bed.

The history of yesterday was written in that small pile.

He recalled the entire adventure.

He spotted the clear green marble when he stepped outside. It was a great start to the day.

He fingered the bottle cap with the free coke symbol that he found in the sand when he went to see if David was coming out.

He wondered why he kept the roofing nail he picked up off the road.

By the post office he collected the three elastic bands and five paper clips.

He played pick-up baseball until about noon when he nipped home for lunch. After a sandwich, he put some cookies in his pocket. That's what all those brown crumbs were.

Terry headed for the lake because there were always neat things to find along the shore.

That old Dare Devil without its hook was by a rock. Maybe he'll put a hook on it some day.

He intended to skip that flat rock until he noticed the small imprint of the clamshell fossil. He searched for some more but didn't find any. That would be one of today's activities.

He knew that shiny piece of yellowy Fool's Gold wasn't worth anything, but he liked the looks of it. He also knew that if he banged it against another rock, it would smell like rotten eggs.

It was just after this that the sun had revealed the young pike, nick-named a hammer-handle, hiding under the log.

He found a quarter shining in the sun by a large rock covered with fresh-water snails.

The broken pencil was the last thing he pocketed.

Terry put the collection in his 'special box', turned off the radio and then put the dirty shorts in the laundry basket.

At the breakfast table, his mom asked, "So, what are your big plans today?"

As he poured milk over his Sugar Crisp, he said, "Oh, I'll probably play scrub with the guys."

Meanwhile, he wondered what wonderful treasures he would pocket today.

A Culinary Connection

It was nearly time to open and I was worried.

I was concerned for two connected reasons: yesterday my master chef, Henri, buried his grandmother who had raised him from infancy; and I was apprehensive that the entrees at The West Bank Experience, Fine French Cuisine, might not be up to standard.

At four o'clock I unlocked the main door knowing most patrons would not arrive until well after seven.

I glanced into the kitchen. It was obvious my portly and usually jovial cook was hurting, as he seemed critical of everything Charles, his apprentice, attempted.

I was about to intercede when a diminutive senior lady entered the foyer.

"Are you open?" she asked.

"Why, yes we are. Won't you come in?"

"I don't know if I should." Her eyes flashed. "It looks expensive." She looked at her hands. "I was just looking for a place to have a quiet cup of tea."

"We can handle that," I invited. "Are you hungry?"

Multi-ringed fingers tightened on the beaded cloth purse.

"Heaven knows I should be," she started, "But ever since Phil's funeral I haven't been able to eat a thing. My stomach just knots up, if you know what I mean."

"How long were you married?" I ventured.

There was a tiny chuckle. "Oh my, I've been a widow for years. No, my grandson was killed in a car crash a few days ago and…."

She began rummaging in her handbag.

I snatched a cloth napkin and handed it to her.

After dabbing her eyes she looked up. "I'm sorry. I shouldn't be bothering you with my troubles."

"Not at all," I said and then gently taking her elbow, I led her to a small table in an isolated corner. "It will be nice and cozy for you here."

I motioned to one of the waiters.

"Would you please bring this lady a pot of tea? I want to talk to Henri."

I hurried into the kitchen where I put my arm around Henri's broad shoulders.

"Henri, my friend, how would you like to apply your personal expertise to a very special customer?"

His immaculate mustache twisted in a quizzical look.

"Don't worry about the menu," I assured him. "It will be slow for a while yet and Charles is quite capable of looking after any customers."

Curiosity showed in Henri's face as I led him to the door.

"Come and meet her."

The elderly woman put down her teacup as we approached.

"Henri," I began, "This is…?"

"Mrs. Harrison," she finished. "Doris Harrison."

"Mrs. Harrison, this is Henri, our master chef."

As they shook hands I addressed Henri. "Mrs. Harrison has not had much of an appetite for the past few days."

I pulled out a chair, indicated for him to sit down, and then I turned to the lady.

"Mrs. Harrison…" I started.

"Doris. Please call me Doris."

"Okay Doris, if anyone can cure a missing appetite it is Henri here. I have to go, but I'll let you explain why you have not been eating."

I patted Henri on the shoulder. "Don't worry about the kitchen."

I went to the back where the staff agreed to steer customers away from that area.

The corner-table drama unfolded. Tentative at first, the two heads soon bent closer. She dabbed her eyes while he patted her hand, then later she dabbed his eyes and patted his hand.

No one dared to refill the teapot.

I was helping Charles with the devilled lobster canapés when Henri, beaming like a little kid, burst into the kitchen.

"Mon Dieu, she is like my own Grandmere! And she is starving! I shall make for her the perfect dinner – Red Snapper with Lemon Marjoram Butter."

Once again Henri was in fine form.

He was soon brushing marjoram butter over two broiled fillets framed by roasted potatoes and baby carrots.

"Some Chablis Grand Cru would go well, eh?" he winked.

I laughed. "I'll get it."

As I poured their wine it was obvious the dinner was secondary to the culinary connection. I left the bottle in the ice bucket.

Much later, as I was assisting Charles with the Cauliflower Crostini hors d'oeuvres, Henri strolled in.

"Helas, she has gone," he sighed, and then wagging his finger he continued, "But you know, I think she will be back."

"Of course," I teased, "She likes your cooking."

Henri remained serious. He took my hand as tears welled in his intense black eyes.

"Thank you, my friend. I shall never forget this."

He continued to hold my hand while I nodded, swallowed hard, and smiled weakly.

Finally he let go and walked over to Charles. "So now, mon ami, how are the lobster canapés coming along?"

A Mashed Myth

Long ago in Roman times, Jupiter noticed the other Gods were bored - just sitting around. He said, "To give them something to do I'll create a special food for mankind. Each God and Goddess can help in his or her own way."

Juno, his wife, said "I'd like to help too, dear. What can I do?"

"While I organize the guys, you contact my sisters, Vesta and Ceres, and then Diana, Venus, Minerva, Maia and Flora and bring them over here."

Juno snorted. "I can understand inviting Maia, Goddess of Growth, and Flora the Goddess of Flowers, but why Diana who looks after the moon?"

"Well," Jupiter shrugged, "Some of you Goddesses can be pretty miserable if you don't get invited to a party. So to keep everyone happy, put Diana with Vesta, who looks after the home, and Venus who is in charge of Love. Remember the happier the home the better the garden."

"And what has Minerva got to do with things?"

"Man cannot cultivate a successful garden without knowledge, and since she is the Goddess of Wisdom, she should be a big asset to your group."

Juno was not impressed and crossed her arms. "Yeah, right!" she snorted, "And just what will you be doing in the meantime?"

"I won't need my brother Neptune for gardening, so I'll have him guide the navigators around the world to distribute the food.

"Once I have Apollo and Saturn working on sunshine and time, I'll have my hands full keeping that feisty Mars and drunken Bacchus from tearing each other apart. I want everything to go smoothly when I create the new food."

With her hands on hips,

Jupiter's wife said, "You know, Jupe, it would be nice to know what we are dealing with here before you go off on another one of your tangents."

"What are you whining about now, Juno? I always know what I am doing."

"Tell that to Jason and his Argonauts! We had to help him out of all sorts of predicaments because of your stupid challenges."

Jupiter frowned. "Well, this time it will be different. The Gods can contribute in their own unique ways. Mankind will like the new food staple. I'll call it an otatop."

"They won't like the name."

"Well," shrugged Jupiter, "Mankind can change it if it wants to. A different title won't change the food value I'm putting into it."

"Okay, fine; now, just what is an otatop?"

Juno's husband bent closer. "It is a vegetable that doesn't need a seed when it is planted. You just bury a piece of an old one. And it will grow almost anywhere, which will be great for settlers clearing land."

"I suppose that will be useful."

"And I'm going to give it lots of carbohydrates for energy. More than that," - Jupiter was on a roll - "I'll make a portion of the internal starch content resistant to enzymatic digestion in the stomach and in the small intestine. The extra fiber will offer protection against colon cancer; improve glucose tolerance and insulin sensitivity; lower plasma cholesterol and triglyceride concentrations; increase satiety; and possibly even reduce fat storage."

"They won't be aware of those things for years," Juno yelled, "Let alone pronounce the names!"

"Hey, that is nothing! My opatops will have vitamin C, vitamin B6, potassium, magnesium, phosphorus,iron, and zinc, along with thiamin, riboflavin, folate, and niacin!"

Juno stared at Jupiter. "What did you do, learn a second language?"

"NO! And I'm also going to make the otatops different colours such as white, red, yellow, brown and a nice purple."

"Why?"

"Oh, I don't know," Jupiter mused. "It will give mankind something to argue about – like which one tastes the best."

Suddenly a litany of voices chimed in. "We have been listening and we like your idea, Jupiter. May we offer some suggestions?"

Flora was first to speak. "I will give your otatop dainty flowers."

"And I will give it lovely large leaves," added Maia, "to catch the sunshine Apollo sends. What about you, Ceres?"

Ceres smiled. "Since Jupiter has so many varieties, I shall create the perfect conditions for each type; from the sandy earth of the flat lands to gravel mountain soils."

"And I will give them time to grow," announced Saturn.

Jupiter smiled. "All of you are very kind. It is terrific when we work together."

Venus interjected. "Cupid and I have been talking. We will work with Vesta and Janus. When there are lots of your otatops, mankind's home will be happier."

"What about you, Minerva?" asked Juno.

"Oh, I shall work behind the scenes by giving man wisdom to know how best to raise otatops."

"Sounds like the project is coming together," boomed Jupiter. "And Bacchus, what do you have in mind?"

"Well, I figure there would be times when mankind will have extra otatops. I'll be working with Diana and Mars to show mankind how to make fantastic vodka."

Jupiter slapped his thigh. "Sounds great!" Turning to Goddess of Wisdom, he asked, "You look a little worried, Minerva; something wrong? Did I forget something?"

She hesitated. "Well, I hate to put a damper on things, but this is a new vegetable. How will it, the otatop know where to grow?"

Jupiter stroked his chin. "You know, I never thought about that. Tell you what I'll do. I'll make sure the otatops can see where they are growing. How is that?"

"I think that about covers everything. What do you think gang?"

There was a chorus of agreement.

"Then that does it," stated Jupiter. "I'll see you all later. Thank you for your help."

The Gods and Goddesses scattered to do their specific tasks. Minerva hung back.

"Okay, Minerva, what is the problem this time?"

"It's the name, Jupiter! Otatop! Who the hell is going to use the term 'otatop'?"

The King of the Gods mused. "I never thought much about it. Well, how about 'potato'?"

"Much better," said Minerva.

My Friend
I Never Met

The water mirrored the bank so perfectly it was difficult to distinguish the transition line.

I enjoyed canoeing near the shore where branches encouraged me with their nearness and sometimes scratching the thwarts.

To pass the time, I played little games such as avoiding a pond flower with the blade, or sliding under a huge leaning tree, or guessing whether the loon ahead would submerge or disdainfully swim out of the way.

Masses of erratic whirligigs dissipate at the bow and reappear astern, while water striders nimbly scampered aside.

It was impossible to determine exactly where one beaver family's territory ended and the next began, but the spacing of their lodges indicated they had delineated the lake into almost equal sections. Freshly skinned branches attested to the health of the inhabitants.

I hadn't spotted any large animals. Warned by the red squirrel's relay system they were probably watching me from some secluded spot.

Periodically, Arctic Terns threatened to skewer me if I came much closer to their island sanctuaries where quite often an osprey nest was piled up in a solitary pine.

The hysterical laugh of loons announced my entry into their spaces where, once in a while, a duck and her flotilla of babies shuffled out of the way.

I was looking forward to hearing the White-Crowned Sparrow's 'too-wee-twee-twee-twee-twee' announcing the end of the day.

That was the great thing about canoeing: one merged with nature.

The angle of the sun told me it was about one o'clock and my watch verified it. My smile vanished when I realized that I had better pick up the tempo if I was to reach Tom's by five. I knew the west end of the lake was at least four hours away, but I was heartened knowing his place was about an hour this side.

After three years of intermittent contact via the jam jar secreted in his woodpile, I was finally going to meet my friend.

I really couldn't blame him for being cautious at first; after all, I could have been one of the people looking for him.

Anticipation gave impetus to my paddle.

It was while hurrying to renew my claims before their expiration date that I stumbled upon Tom.

Cutting across that open stretch, without reading the clouds, had not been one of my brightest moments. The three-foot whitecaps produced by the sudden headwind made me kneel in the canoe, equalize the supplies, and aim for a tiny spit about a mile away.

An eternity later, as I entered the land's influence, the waves began abating.

I angled toward a grove of cedars.

My arms and back begged for relief. I certainly was not eager for the usual penetrating scramble so I aimed for a dark area that often indicated a rare break in the wall.

Summoning up a last bit of energy, I powered into the trees.

The anticipated crunch never materialized. I was both surprised and thrilled when I sailed into a secluded lagoon.

There was no time to savour the moment. Although I was not looking forward to tenting in a windstorm, I shoved the pack-sacks under the overturned canoe. It was not a time to be choosy. I grabbed the bungee-bag and looked for a fairly flat area for the tent.

Just as I was about to lay out the tent, I noticed a faint path leading up the hill. Since one can imagine all sorts of things in the bush when the light fades, I looked more closely. It was definitely a trail.

A skyward glance indicated the storm was at least a half an hour off, so I figured there would be enough time to see where it went.

I headed uphill.

Just over the rise and blending into the forest was a log cabin. The area around it was untouched, which added to the seclusion of the place. From the height of the undergrowth, I estimated the cabin must have been there for at least ten years.

I could tell a great deal of time and effort had gone into building it. A stovepipe with its dispersal cap protruded through a debris-cleared roof.

The door had been wired shut from the outside.

I peeked though the window, but only the counter under the window was discernible.

A strong gust roared through the trees. Down the hill I heard a sheekoe – a dead tree - crash and another one crunched down off to my left.

It was certainly no night to be in a tent.

In the bush there is an unwritten rule: In an emergency, you may use a stranger's cabin. The corollary to this is: you must not damage anything; in fact, you must leave it the same, or better, than you found it.

I ran down the hill, stuffed the fly and tent under the canoe, and grabbed the pack-sack and the nap-sack. By the time I was back up the hill, the lightning and thunder were almost simultaneous. The rain-wall chased me into the cabin where I slammed the door and leaned back against it.

The lightning flashes showed a kerosene lamp suspended over a small table. I soon had its warm glow illuminating the room.

I retrieved and lit my own propane lantern and then turned off the other one.

'No point using up my friend's fuel,' I muttered, and then I wondered why I had used the term 'friend'.

I surveyed my refuge. It was basic but what else would one need out here. Red and white checked oilcloth covered the table and the counter under the window.

Opposite the window a small bed nestled between the adjacent wall and a woodpile by the door. Huddled in its heat shield a neat cast iron stove promised a warmer future.

A fire soon had the cabin feeling cozy. The limited wood supply indicated there was a larger supply elsewhere. When I brought some sticks in from the covered stack by the door outside, I made a mental note to replace the pieces and the kindling in the morning.

After putting a couple of substantial pieces into the firebox, I adjusted the damper.

From a stream of water pouring off the roof I filled a wide enamelled pot and put it on the stove. One can always use hot water.

A stomach twinge made me realize I hadn't eaten for hours. I set up my camp stove and started a pot of water for the Kraft Dinner.

My watch indicated it was also time to start thinking about turning in.

I laid the ground sheet on the bed and unrolled the sleeping bag over it. My sweater would have to do for a pillow.

Mosquitoes, energized by the cabin's warmth, began to make their presence known. I lit a mosquito repellent coil and put it on a tin plate by the stove.

I poured some boiling water over my tea bag, stirred in the pasta, and set it to cook over a reduced flame.

It was while relaxing with my tea I finally had the opportunity to look around the cabin.

The pots and pans hung on the walls and a variety of clothing on nails. A little cupboard sported dishes and utensils. Since there was no hurry, I laid back and surveyed the now well-lit room.

What kind of person was my unknown host?

Perhaps he was a trapper. This idea was dismissed because the number and variety of traps plus drying racks should be much larger.

Maybe he was a prospector. This notion did not stand up either. From what I tell, the rocks along the window sill seemed to have been collected more for interest than for value.

Everything appeared quite normal, and yet something was missing.

The answer eluded me.

The window frame was lined with newspaper clippings. I'd look at them in the morning while I did the dishes.

Rather than finish the Kraft Dinner, I ate a few cookies.

I dissuaded myself from having a second cup of tea knowing I would not feel like getting up in the middle of the night.

The flashing and crashing had subsided indicating the storm front had passed leaving the dull drumming of the rain.

The sleeping bag was looking better all the time.

I put two logs on the bed of coals, topped up the water pot and then closed the damper.

A visit to Mother Nature was last.

With the cabin nice and toasty, I shucked off my heavy shirt and pants, switched on the flashlight and turned off the lantern.

After crawling in I put the flashlight within easy reach before turning it off.

The intensity of the darkness was disconcerting, but gradually the outline of the window became distinguishable.

To tell how far away the storm was, I began to count the seconds between the lightning flashes and the thunder: One thousand, two thousand, three thousand, four thousand, five thou....

A tiny clink-plink woke me.

In its white vest and grey 'dinner jacket' a delicate deer mouse was enjoying the Kraft dinner remnants.

It did not scamper away when I put two more pieces of wood into the stove.

"That should hold things until morning," I told the mouse as I lit another mosquito coil.

I crawled back in and dozed off again knowing there would be one stuffed furry friend sleeping in his bed tonight.

The sharp repetitive cry of a Pileated Woodpecker penetrated my senses. The amount of daylight streaming through the window indicated it was a beautiful day.

I crawled out into the cool cabin. The few residual coals ignited the wood chips I threw in. After revisiting Mother Nature, I smiled at the table for it was obvious the mouse had called his friends because all the scraps were gone.

A shave was going to feel refreshing. From the large pot I poured some warm water into a blue enamelled wash basin.

The mirror beside the window reflected a scruffy but well-rested face. I lathered up. During the mindless chore of shaving, my eyes perused the few old newspaper clippings.

I forgot about shaving.

A chill ran up my spine.

With a bit of mental effort I put them into a sequential order. They spoke of informants, governmental corruption, the mafia, a bungled witness protection programme, a murdered family, hung juries and a case dismissed due to lack of evidence, mainly the mysterious disappearance of the star witness, rumoured to have been 'eliminated'.

On top of the tiny cupboard was a photo of a two young boys standing in front of an attractive lady. The paper had mentioned a woman and two children.

Had I stumbled upon someone attempting to disappear?

The more I thought about the location: the impenetrable cedar shoreline, the secluded lagoon, the invisible trail, the cabin blending into the forest, the more nervous I became.

It was obvious my host did not want to be found.

A few swipes finished off the whiskers.

I scrubbed the plate, pot and utensils, dried them and returned them to their original places. I used my face cloth to wipe down the table and counter. I dribbled enough wash-water to put out the coals without soaking the stove.

The word pack sack took on a whole new meaning as I threw my belongings into it. After a cursory glance around the room, I rewired the door, and hurried towards the canoe.

I stopped.

"I can't leave like this!" I announced to the trees. "He'll know I've been here!"

On a page ripped out of my prospector's notebook, I described my accidental discovery of his cabin. I thanked him for the use and safety of his cabin; that I had burned about ten pieces of wood; and that I would really like to pop in on my way back to thank him.

I signed my name, hesitated, and then added: "Your secret is safe with me."

I enclosed a twenty-dollar bill and put the note in an empty jar.

Outside I slipped the jar under the top logs in the woodpile, and then rewired the door.

A few hours of paddling did little to suppress the many questions swirling around in my mind. What have I got myself into? Should I stay out of it? Should I meet him? Was he dangerous? Who was this man? How did he arrive here? How does he obtain supplies? I knew this system of lakes intersected the Canadian Pacific Railway line. Perhaps he had special arrangements with the C.P.R. Budd Car on specific days?

I did not sleep well at the intermediate campsite.

It was late the next afternoon and several portages later that I made camp on my claim.

Although reblazing claim lines and retagging the posts occupied the daily routine, it was while sitting by the campfire that thoughts of 'my host' returned and delayed much needed sleep.

I collected and labelled some samples for which I hoped would receive high assays.

It was near the end of the fifth day, when I had the strangest feeling of being watched. I looked around fully expecting to see someone.

I laughed. No one knew I was here.

With the necessary work completed, I returned to the campsite about mid-afternoon to label and record the latest samples.

When I reached for my notebook I found the pen was between the pages.

'Strange,' I mused, 'I always hook my pen on top of the page I am working on. Oh well. I probably just threw it inside this morning.'

I stuck my head out the door.

'You're getting Prospector's Paranoia.'

Later on, when I went to dip some water from the nearby spring, I saw the distinct indentation of a canoe keel.

It was recent landing because the groove still had fairly sharp edges.

Someone had been here!

Obviously, they were long gone, but I still found myself looking around. I wasn't worried about being claim-jumped because all my posts were tagged and noted.

Unanswered questions gnawed.

It was a long night. It seemed as if every normal forest noise awoke me. Finally around four o'clock I fell into an exhausted sleep.

The crash of pots startled me. A small bear was rummaging around by the fire pit. I must have presented a terrible sight because he ran off as soon as he saw me. If I looked the way I felt, I wouldn't want to be around me either.

I didn't bother shaving. Breakfast was a disaster. The bacon fat caught fire and ruined the eggs. I dumped the mess into the fireplace, and consoled myself with a peanut butter sandwich and spring water.

I kept looking up and around while striking camp.

Nothing seemed to fold properly, or pack easily. The canoe looked as if a complete amateur loaded it. Oh well, I'd reorganize it tonight at the halfway campsite.

I pushed off.

After an hour or so I was resolved to take my chances and would attempt to meet 'my host'. I mentally rehearsed various methods of asking questions; ways of introducing myself; and means of approaching the cabin.

My determination was reflected in my paddling because I suddenly discovered I was expending far too much energy. It was if I was trying to reach the cabin by tonight - a physical impossibility — as it was another day and a half away, and that was not counting all the portages.

Cruising close to an island I coasted and took a long welcome drink from the canteen, while I looked around.

Just as the island blocked my view I saw something 'different' by the shore about a mile away. I tried to reverse, but the extra weight made it difficult. It seemed to take forever to return to the point where I thought I had seen someone or something. I stared. Nothing. I scanned the far shore. Still nothing. Was it my heightened state of awareness that made me imagine it? It was a possibility and yet....

The first of three portages was still an hour ahead. Since I was stopped, I decided to have a bite to eat. I swung in, tied up to a tree, grabbed the packsack, climbed the little hill and deliberately found a comfortable spot from where I could watch the far shore.

I took my time with a thick honey sandwich and a stack of cookies washed down with spring water.

There was nothing there.

The angle of the sun said it was time to go if I was to make the island campsite below the third rapids.

After putting the cookie bag within arms reach, I shoved off, pointed the prow at gap at the east end where I could shoot the first rapids.

It was after seven when I made camp. The portaging had taken more time due to the rock samples.

As soon as I slipped through the entrance, I knew he wasn't home. His canoe wasn't there and the dog didn't bark.

I hurried up the hill to find the door wired shut.

I peeked through the window. Everything was pretty much as I remembered it.

A quick search located the jam-jar.

The note, in excellent handwriting, was inside:

I am glad the cabin served

as a shelter for you.

Please be careful. Things

are not what they seem.

Tom, a friend.(Over).

I flipped the paper.

Good luck with your claim.

You may be interested in

some long crystals along

the shore about a mile

south from where you are.

Look for a black dyke in

pink and brown granite.

Son-of-a-gun! He had been at my campsite! But of course! He must know this region like the back of his hand.

On a page from my book I wrote:

Thank you for telling me

who was at my camp.

I wish you had stayed

but I understand your

hesitancy. Hope everything

is all right. I put

some surplus supplies

inside. Canned ham is

quite good. Take care.
We'll shake hands one
of these days. Cheers.
Your friend, Jack.
Next summer.

I piled my extra foodstuffs on the table. Since there was no need to rush off, I looked around the area. One path led to a boxed-in spring, while another led in the opposite direction to an open-sided outhouse. An oil drum had been converted into a smoke oven.

I put my perishables into his cooler.

With a heavy heart I headed for home, as it would be at least another year before I could return.

The fall and winter months were occupied with teaching; completing a research paper; and securing the best options for my claims.

I was looking forward to the summer when I could complete the annual assessment work; the possible staking what I figured was a tourmaline outcrop; and most importantly, popping in and finally - I glanced at the Reader's Digests I had collected - meeting Tom.

With the school year behind me, I ensured that the necessary papers and tags were in order. I also acquired the geological survey map with the south connection onto mine.

I chuckled as I paddled because I was noticing the same fallen trees, beaver houses, nests, and quite possibly the same lake residents.

Again I was disappointed, but not entirely surprised, to find the canoe gone and no barking welcoming committee. I shrugged; after all Tom had no idea when I might show up.

The jam-jar note read:

Have gone to meet the

Budd Car for supplies.

It seems like I have

better luck with the

train than with you,

my friend. We will meet

one of these days.

The ham was fantastic!

Thank you. Tom

On the back of his sheet I wrote:

Sorry I missed you again.

I have left some reading

materials. I'll be looking

for those crystals, will

tell you what happened

when we meet.

Your friend, Jack.

The long summer sunsets were appreciated as it was quite late when I crawled into another quickly erected tent. There would be time tomorrow to settle in.

I slept soundly knowing there would be no strangers prowling around.

In the morning I was too tired to attempt any bush work, so I set up the fire pit, collected wood, re-established the cooler in the spring, and extended the fly over the working area.

Two days were spent reflagging the boundaries, labelling the posts and recording it all as required. While making a more detailed sketch map of the claim, I was pleased to find another chalcopyrite showing in the northeast quadrant, which meant the ore-body was larger than I first estimated.

With the Department of Mines requirements fulfilled, I relaxed in my hammock while I studied the new map for the next day's expedition.

The squirrels were glad to receive their usual morning treat of peanut butter on a cookie before I pushed off and headed south.

I scrutinized the east shoreline. About two miles south I saw a narrow black dyke slicing through pink-white granite formation, and soon located the tourmaline crystals nestling in a grey-white dyke of aplite.

By late afternoon I finished staking one claim. I double-checked that the witness posts at the water's edge were properly done.

With the work completed, I collected good samples of tourmaline and headed back to the campsite.

The next morning, while relaxing with the registration papers, I was suddenly faced with a dilemma. To register the claim I needed Tom's last name. More to the point, the claim would bring attention to him.

I would have to talk to him.

It was late the next day when I slipped through the cedar entrance to discover his canoe gone. I hurried up the hill to find the jam-jar.

Dear Jack

Was unsure of your return,
pantry was getting low,
gone hunting a day or so
from here, hope I'm back
before you read this, am
looking forward to
meeting you. Tom

On the back of his note I replied

Sorry we missed each
other again. We certainly
have bad timing. I staked
out a claim on the
tourmaline crystals.
Thanks for the tip. I'll be
back next summer with
any developments. Keep
well. Your friend, Jack.

After leaving surplus supplies on the table, I made a final glance at the cabin and pushed off.

Life was routine until a new flurry of media reports described the final conviction of some high-ranking politicians and their underworld cronies. Background information was reviewed. Old police reports regarding the unsolved murder of the family of the agent who had revealed the corruption in the first place.

I was underway by eight the next morning and by one

o'clock the patch of cedars was in sight. I was hoping my friend would be home this time so that we could meet and shake hands at last.

Slipping through secret entrance, I pulled up the canoe and hurried to where the message jar was hidden.

Inside was a scrawled note:
I am glad the cabin served
as a shelter for you and
thank you for leaving
everything as you found it.
Please be careful. Things
are not what they seem.
Your friend Tom

I was really disappointed.
On the back of his note I wrote:
I am sorry I missed you
again. Hope everything
is all right. I put some
supplies I did not need
just inside the door. The
canned ham is quite good.
Take care. We'll shake hands
one of these days. Cheers.
Your friend, Jack.

After putting the extra supplies inside the cabin I pushed off for home. It was a long sad paddle back to the end of the lake where my Land Rover was parked

Since it would be quite a while before I returned to that

particular lake system, I spent the time looking for a mining company that would option my claims.

Life became routine until a flurry of media reports purported the final conviction of high-ranking politicians and their underworld cronies. Background information was recalled, but I was especially interested in the old police reports regarding the unsolved murders of the family of the agent who had revealed the corruption in the first place.

The name of the agent was Tom Barker.

My heart froze. Could my unknown friend be that 'Tom'?

It would still be many months till summer released the lakes from their icy grip, but I was determined to find out.

So here I was - a bit apprehensive I suppose - paddling towards an uncertain rendezvous.

Finally, I swung my canoe through the hidden slot in the cedars. I was not surprised there was no canoe, but I was chilled at the indefinable atmosphere I felt.

I hurried up the cabin where I found the door ajar.

Although everything seemed to be in its place, nothing had been used in many months. The mouse had succeeded in chewing a hole into the Kraft Dinner box and the crackers had been raided.

Yet something was missing; something had changed.

It was the window! All the clippings were gone as were the pictures.

There was an ominous atmosphere about the place.

After a frenetic scramble I found the jar and the note.

Thank you for being

so trustworthy.
Keep well, my friend.
Don't look for me.
Tom.

It was a long paddle home.

Life in a Leaf

A loon's serenade drifted down the lake as the autumn sunset deepened.

With toes prodding floating leaves, a grandfather and his twelve-year-old grandson sat on the end of a dock. The cottage visit was over, so they were savouring the last moments.

There wasn't much to say. It had all been said. Neither wanted to say goodbye.

The old man reached down, picked up a large maple leaf and spun it by the stem. "You know, Jerry, they say a whole lifetime is written in a leaf."

"What do you mean, Grandpa?"

"Here, you hold it. This stem leads to the main vein. We might call it the thread of life."

The boy's finger traced the rib-line. "It's the thickest one."

"What do you notice about it as it reaches the top?"

"It gets thinner."

"So we could say life starts out very strong, like down here and, as time passes, a person becomes more selective, more focused."

"I guess people want a lot of stuff at first."

Grandpa's eyes sparkled. "Good point. Now, Grandson, what else do you notice in the leaf?"

"There are lines coming from the middle one."

"Yes, and just as these veins support the leaf, people grow, go to school, make friends, have families and perhaps start businesses that branch out. Many experiences shape life."

"You can see all that?"

The old man chuckled. "Well, as one gets older, one becomes philosophical; you think about the past."

"I suppose so," the boy nodded, "but I don't have much of a past yet."

"That's true, but you will."

The loon's call echoed the sentiments.

"This leaf sure has a lot of different colours, Grandpa."

"Now that you mention it, it does have all the hues you find in leaves. In fact, they could represent an entire lifetime."

The grandpa glanced at his grandson who had become quiet. "I'm sorry, Grandson, I did not mean to be a downer."

"No, no, Grandpa, I like listening to you! Tell me about the colours."

"Let's do it together. Perhaps we can give them names without using 'colour' names."

A wrinkled finger pointed at an area nearest the base. "What do you think of when you see this shade?"

"Springtime, when the leaves first come out."

"So what name can we give it without calling it light green?"

"How about 'New'?or 'Beginning'? How about 'New Beginning'?"

"Sounds good to me," smiled Grandpa. "Life is just starting out. Everything is bright and fresh. Now, as we get further out, the colour becomes darker and deeper. Any ideas?"

"This is the colour of summer leaves. Let's call it 'Summer Time'."

"That name fits as well as any I can think of."

"Yeah, and the person is growing and learning."

The old man gently squeezed his grandson's shoulder. "You're pretty sharp."

A self-conscious smile creased the lad's face. "Too bad the 'Summer Time' colour doesn't stay." The boy's finger brushed the leaf. "Right here it changes to the fall shades like now."

"Have you ever heard the term: The Autumn of One's Life?"

The boy nodded.

"Well, what part of life could this tint represent?

"Probably the time when the person is much older. Maybe he has a family, a good job, and things like that."

"Right," the elderly man beamed at his grandson, "And he is probably looking forward to retiring. So, now give that shade a name."

The boy scratched his chin. "How about 'Autumn', or 'Pumpkin', or 'Campfire'? How about 'Autumn Campfire'?"

"I like it. So, now moving further out, we see our 'Autumn Campfire' changes to a red and then to brown.

A young finger ran over the leaf. "Yeah, but we can't use reddish brown. How about 'Northern Sunset'?"

"Beautiful! The sunset of life! So what is the person like now?"

"Oh, he would be old, kinda like…." The boy stopped.

"Like what?"

The lad looked at his hands, and then muttered, "L-like you, Grandpa."

"That's right! In a way, it is a great time of life. I can look back and be thankful for many things, especially for my wonderful grandson."

"I suppose so."

The man continued. "So now, we are away out here at the edge where it is dark, ragged and crumbly. Can you think of colour-name for this area?"

The leaf was flung onto the lake.

"I know what it means, Grandpa, and I am not naming that colour!"

Silence descended as toes prodded leaves.

A youthful hand crept across and took hold of the wrinkled one. "I don't want you to die, Grandpa."

The old man squeezed the boy's hand. "Thank you, Grandson. I have to stick around to watch you grow up, don't I?"

A loon's moan drifted down the lake.

"How about we go in for a hot chocolate."

"I'd like that."

Medicinal Mud

Somehow the visit to my wife's gravesite was much more difficult this morning. Oh, I told her how much I missed her; mentioned the kids and the grandkids; and rattled on about how her cat was finally accepting me - no effort on his part.

Meanwhile, my fingers cleared the debris from last night's thunderstorm.

I rose to go home, but I couldn't move. Icouldnot move. I did not want to go home. It wasn't a home any more; it was an empty shell.

My lips quivered as I remembered how we had struggled and persevered to build that house and raise our family.

The kids still call to see how I am doing. I could hear them now: "Dad, it's been over a year now. You have to get out more, not just to visit Mom and back."

What the hell do they know!

"All right," I shouted at the sky, "I'm out. I'M OUT!"

The town's neglected graveyard nestled against the forest looked so forlorn. Glaring at the trees, I strode through the cemetery and ploughed into the bush where, after an eternity of mindless thrashing and crashing, I stumbled into a clearing.

"Idiot," I gasped with my hands on my knees. "Good way to give yourself a coronary."

As my breathing settled, I realized I was on an old gravel road the forest was inexorably reclaiming. Various shrubs lined the route while aspens formed a cosy yellow-green arch.

The peace was overwhelming. I had forgotten how wonderful it was to wander in the bush where the burdens of life were dispelled by the serenity.

Laura would have loved it here. God, I miss her.

Using a stick to poke at things as I followed the trail, I was startled when the road ended at the rim of an abandoned gravel pit. After last night's storm, it was like gazing upon a diorama of the Canadian Shield. The old excavation was a myriad of tiny lakes interconnected by small streams, with grassy areas resembling the forest.

I picked my way down to a flat boulder that provided a rather comfortable seat upon which to savour some boyhood memories.

I remembered the endless black spruce that stood where the foot-deep moss was used to build forts near long-forgotten frog ponds.

I visualized walking through fresh undisturbed puddles where the fine silt oozed up between my toes. I felt them instinctively curl inside my shoes.

With the sun on my back, I closed my eyes and allowed nostalgia to comfort me.

"Hi, mister."

A sharp, clear voice shattered my reverie.

Bare feet and tanned, bony legs extended from a pair of Khaki shorts and a loose red-striped T-shirt. Looking up I saw the sun-bleached, curly head of a six- or-seven-year-old boy beaming at me.

I returned the smile.

"Hi there yourself, young man."

"Whacha doing out here?"

I mentally shrugged. Logical question; why would an old fart like me be sitting out in the middle of a gravel pit?

"Dreaming, just dreaming."

"About what?"

Persistence: thy name is boy.

There was an unpretentious honesty in his eyes, so I answered him.

"Well, if you must know, I was dreaming about mud."

I was hoping the tone of my voice would deter further conversation - perhaps indicate how I wished to be alone in my misery.

The face was still there.

"Yeah, mud's great, ain'tit! Did you ever walk in puddles when you were a kid?"

"Er, yes, as a matter of fact...."

"Do you wanna walk in the puddles with me?"

His boyish exuberance was infectious. Instinctively, part of me said, Don't be silly! But a more adventurous sector said, GO FOR IT!

"Aw, what the hell," I laughed, "Why not?"

I shrugged off my jacket, slipped off my shoes and socks, and rolled up my pants.

"I know the really good ones," he said, flitting about as I put my things in a neat pile. "They don't have any glass in them. You hafta watch out for glass, you know."

The kid was right. I had quite forgotten about that hazard.

"Thank you very much," I said as I stood up.

The boy headed towards the puddles. Perhaps I wasn't fast enough because he kept glancing back.

"Hang on; I'm coming…er…what's your name?"

"Michael. Kids call me Mike. What's yours?"

"Andrew. Just call me Andy."

Laura always called me Andy, except when she was angry with me.

"Do you want your own?" he asked.

"My own what?"

"Puddles!" The question was simple enough, but he repeated it. "Do you want your own puddles?"

"Well, I don't know." I was confused. How do you own a puddle?

I smiled as Michael strode towards me.

With hands on his hips, and in the voice of a long-suffering parent, he instructed, "I know what puddles are safe ones. So, I can show you your puddles, and I can have my puddles, if that's what you want."

Perhaps it was something in his voice - or the body language - that indicated he wanted to share the time-honoured tradition of puddle walking.

"How about we do the puddles together," I suggested. "That way, both of us can enjoy all the puddles."

He whooped and raced to the nearest one.

"Can't go in that one," he said, pointing at a harmless-looking one. "Someone broke a bottle off that rock. Mom was really mad when I cut my foot."

"Bet your dad wasn't too pleased either," I said.

Instantly his little face changed.

"Don't have no dad," said a subdued voice. "He died."

Oh God!

"I'm very sorry. I didn't know...."

I certainly did not want to pursue the topic.

I should comfort him.

As if anticipating my intensions, he skipped off to the first puddle.

"Here we go."

Waving his scrawny arms to maintain balance, Michael gingerly proceeded down the slippery slope.

"Ooooooh, it feels real mushy!"

Being a step or two behind I asked, "Do you want me to hold your hand in case you fall?"

I knew I shouldn't have said that as soon as the words were out.

His quick 'no-thanks' glance confirmed it.

The wonderfully soft cool ooziness was a soothing ointment for my soul – bliss, absolute bliss.

If Laura could see me now.

"Drunk driver," stated a dull voice.

"What? I'm sorry, Mike. I wasn't listening."

"Drunk driver," he repeated, viciously kicking the water. "My dad was killed by a drunk driver three weeks ago."

He is truly hurting. Perhaps he would talk about it - try to express his feelings.

I was about to suggest it, but he scampered off and waited for me at the next soupy adventure. This time though, as we started to squish our way across, he slipped his hand into mine.

The little hand was comforting.

"That mud feels wonderful," I sighed.

"Sure does."

In self-imposed silence we continued through the puddles.

"You married?"

His question startled me.

"Yes, I mean, I was."

"Oh."

We savoured more puddles; his little hand guided me through the safe ones.

"Did she die?"

The question was an arrow.

"Yes. My beautiful Laura died about a year ago."

"Oh."

Again, we retreated into our feelings. The mud and puddles enhanced long-stifled emotions.

My vision blurred.

"Betcha miss her, huh."

The kid is killing me!

"Very much."

After a long pause I heard, "Yeah, I know."

Neither of us was moving.

"Married forty years," I blubbered.

I attempted to suppress the rising caldron of anguish, swallowed hard, and covered my mouth with the back of my hand.

Suddenly, the child let out a heart-rending wail, and clamped onto my waist!

"I miss my dad. I MISS MY DAD!"

Automatically, I hugged his shaking body to mine.

"I miss my Laura! I MISS MY LAURA!"

A year of squelched agony wrenched itself free. Torrents of anger and loneliness drained into the puddle.

Time stood still. Our tears and fears merged with the water, while the deep mud comforted our souls and consoled our hurting hearts.

I gradually realized I was holding onto the lad for a bit of support.

Eventually, his little arms relaxed and dropped.

When he stepped back, we glanced sheepishly - yet unashamedly - at each other.

I was certain my face was as tear-stained as his.

He smiled weakly.

"Thanks, mister."

"No, thank you, young man," I said and handed him some tissues from the packet I always carried. "I needed that."

"Me too."

We giggled as we wiped our eyes.

He took in a long deep shuddering breath.

We hugged again - tenderly this time.

"Do you want half a peanut butter sandwich?" he asked as he stepped back and looked towards the meeting-rock. "It's in my bag over there."

"Sure," I said, "And we'll split the chocolate bar I have in my coat, although it might be a bit soft."

"We can lick the paper."

In the soft afternoon breeze we quietly shared our rations, while bird songs completed the magic.

I felt rejuvenated.

I could see that he also felt better.

Reconciliation replaced conversation.

"I'm afraid I didn't bring anything to drink." My voice seemed louder than necessary.

"Oh, that's okay," he said, and pointed across the pit. "We can have a drink from a spring just down the hill there."

This kid's a lifesaver, in more ways than one.

Again silence settled on our lunch rock.

"I guess you'll want to go home now, huh?" It was more statement than question.

I didn't respond immediately because, remarkably enough, I did feel like going home.

"Yes, I suppose so," I said, "but there's no hurry. Actually, I was hoping we could do some more puddles, if that's what you want."

I was rewarded with a gorgeous smile.

"I'd like that."

We continued to absorb reality as we stared across the pit. Then slowly – unconsciously - his little hand came to rest upon my knee.

"Nice day for puddles, eh Andy?"

I covered his hand with mine, and gently squeezed it.

"Great, Mike, just great.

The Old Shoe

I did not want to go home, not yet anyway. I knew I'd have to eventually, but in a vain attempt to delay the inevitable, I'd puttered around the office.

My little business was doing not too badly, growing slowly, but it had stagnated lately.

I left a message that I'd be late – didn't happen that often - I was usually home in time for supper with the wife and kids.

In the washroom I wiped my face with a cool damp cloth. Tired angry eyes stared back from the mirror.

Damn kids! It was always the damn kids the wife and I argued over. It happened again this morning: school or homework or rap-music or chores or whatever. There should be a law that locks teenagers up until they are twenty when their brains come back! I don't think I was miserable to my parents. When I was growing up, we kids were well mannered, obeyed the rules, and were respectful.

I plunked into my high-backed office chair.

Sharon keeps telling me to relax. Easy for her to say! I wish I were as laid back as she is. How can I relax while worrying about my little company with the same clients and the same bottom line? Nothing seems to change!

She was usually right, and yet, I continue to argue with her! It must be the male thing to do.

I kicked myself mentally.

As I threw on my overcoat I snapped at the reflection in the hall mirror. "Well, I'll go home when I'm darn good and ready."

I opened the door and glanced down the street.

I'll grab a sandwich at that deli down there. It has a liquor license. A brew will go down real good right about now.

I slammed the office door, locked it and walked down the few stairs into the night.

I hadn't taken three steps when I half-twisted my ankle on something. When I saw it was an old shoe, I kicked it down the sidewalk.

"May I please have my shoe back?"

I jumped. The voice came from inside a large cardboard box beside the wall.

A tired grizzled face emerged. "That was my shoe. It must have fallen off. I apologize for it being in your way."

The mild manner and cultured tones dissuaded any thoughts of retaliation. I retrieved the shoe, which was of fine quality.

"Sorry," I said, handing it to the man. "I've had...." I was about to say that I had a rather tough day, but the sight of the long scruffy fingers reaching for the shoe dispelled any such notion.

I hovered as if something else should follow the exchange.

"Thank you very much, sir. I'd be lost without it. It's been in the family for years." The smile was weak. His eyes twinkled as they met mine, but in that instant I saw wit and intelligence.

My own day-to-day irritants vanished behind an onslaught of questions.

"I do not wish to impose upon you further," the voice continued, "but may I trouble you for a couple of dollars towards a sandwich and a cup of coffee."

"Of course," I said, reaching for my wallet, all the while thinking, 'Two bucks won't go too far.'

"Better than that," I announced a little too loudly, "Let's go into that deli there, and I'll treat you to supper, dessert and everything! I haven't had anything yet myself. What do you say?"

The figure began to shrink back into the box.

'Oh, man!' I scolded myself. 'Obviously he would feel embarrassed going into the restaurant.'

"I'm very sorry. Please forgive my stupidity. I certainly did not mean to embarrass you."

I received a small dismissal wave.

Attempting to redeem myself I offered, "Tell you what. What would you say to my picking up some takeout. We can eat up in my office where it is private, just the two of us?"

I hoped I did not sound too like a kid with a new friend.

The little hand-wave was more definite this time. Taking the gesture as one of affirmation, I stated, "I'll be right back."

I trotted over to the Chinese restaurant where I ordered dinner for three. I glanced towards the cardboard box while I grabbed plastic utensils, napkins, and condiments. There was coffee in the office.

I gave the owner a good tip for rushing the order.

Almost giddy I announced to opening in the box. "I'm back! I hope you are as hungry as I am," I smiled as I edged towards the door. "Shall we go in where it is a little more comfortable?"

It seemed like ages before he emerged from his box.

Suddenly he ducked back in, but then reappeared clutching something wrapped in a blanket.

I led the way into the entryway. Apprehension flashed across his face when I closed the door.

"Sorry about the mess," I apologized while depositing the bags on the desk. "Business has been a bit slow lately."

'Slow?' I thought. 'Damn near stagnant!'

"Life insurance isn't what it used to be. Online advertising and the telemarketers have replaced the personal touch. Used to be one client would recommend you to another."

I knew I was rattling in an attempt to maintain a friendly atmosphere.

"Computer age," he stated softly.

"Yeah, there seems to be more and more of them all the time. I have one for the bookkeeping."

"There is more to computers than accounting."

"I Never got used to them."

I felt foolish.

"These days, you have to keep ahead," the man stated. "Or at least attempt to stay even."

Looking up from unpacking the numerous dishes, I discovered him looking at my certificates and diplomas on the walls.

"Ever thought of diversifying?"

"Well, no."

"It says here, you have a background in economics, especially bonds."

"Well, yes. I specialized in the market for my own interest. I just never...."

"You probably have a solid base of clients who trust you." He looked at me. "Why not become a market consultant?"

"I don't know. I just never…."

"You probably know if they have some resources they might invest. With your background in market fluctuations, you could recommend specific stocks and bonds which would result in substantial returns, for a service fee of course."

"Of course."

My mind raced. 'How come he knows so much about finances?'

I asked him.

"Remember the Rupert-Drummond scandal a few years back?" he said as he flopped onto the settee.

"Well, sort of," I said. "It was a fraud case where one partner skipped out of the country leaving the other to take the rap."

"That's the one. Well, I'm Drummond."

His eyes searched mine for the expected accusation.

My surprise must have shown. "But you were cleared!"

"Yes, after two years." said the defeated voice, "But, it's pretty hard to overcome entrenched perceptions."

"The courts proved you knew nothing about your partner's shenanigans!"

"You can't stop people believing what they want to believe."

He was wilting quickly.

"But," I asked as my eyes looked towards the street, "How did you wind up…?"

"In the box?"

I nodded.

"Long story.Lawyers fees and a defaulted mortgage took everything. After years of trying to re-establish oneself, and a messy divorce, one eventually gives up." He clutched the package more tightly. "But one keeps holding onto dreams."

"By the way," I offered, "My name is Gerald, Gerald Fornier. Call me Gerry."

"I'm Phillip, or Phil, or whatever," he yawned.

"Perhaps we could work together on something," I suggested.

"Perhaps." It was almost a whisper.

Nipping into the back, I called out, "I'll make a fresh pot of coffee. It won't take long. My coffee-making skills have improved since I have been spending more time in the office."

I hoped my chatter was maintaining an upbeat mood. Meanwhile I began wondering if Phillip and I could work together. Could I trust him? Would he trust me?

Re-entering the office I saw Phillip curled up on the couch. His deep breathing, punctuated by little snores, indicated he was in a sound sleep.

The closet shelf yielded a blanket. As covered him, his package thumped onto the carpet. When I picked it up it felt like a laptop. A quick peek verified my suspicion. As I replaced it under his hand, I wondered what secrets it held.

Suddenly all my problems seemed insignificant. Compared to the sleeping figure, what did I have to complain about? I had a good job that, with a bit of consistent effort on my part, would grow. I had a modest house practically paid for. My two kids were probably normal as far as normalcy can be gauged in teenagers. I had a great little wife....

'SHARON!'

The wall-clock showed ten forty-five! She will be worried sick! I raced into the backroom, closed the door and dialled the second phone. Finally, the daughter answered.

"Hi, Melanie," I rushed. "Let me talk to your mom, please - Yes, I know it's late - Yes, everything is fine."

'Well, it was and it wasn't, but how do you explain a situation to which you have inadvertently committed yourself.'

"Er, hi, Honey - Yes, I'm fine - Yes, I'm still at the office - No, I haven't had supper yet."

Heaven knows I had enough food!

"Er, look, something's happened - No, no, the car is fine - Well, it's really hard to explain right now because even I don't know how - No, it's not work. It's - it's - hang on a second."

I opened the door a crack. Phillip had not moved. I ran back to the phone.

"It's all right. He's still sleeping – Phillip - He fell asleep before we could eat - He's a guy I met tonight - At the bottom of the stairs – Well, actually he was in a big cardboard box - No, I don't know how he got there - No, I don't think he is dangerous - Actually, I think we may be working together on a new business venture - I'm trying to explain, Honey, there was this old shoe - ."

Mitten Memories

Abandoned and forsaken, wet and dirty, the mitten was slowly being released from the shrinking snow bank.

After wringing it out, it lay in my hand like a dead bird - a forgotten dream - a lost child. Childhood innocence emanated from the dulled pinks, whites and blues of the variegated yarn.

As I stared at it, my heart saddened.

I envisioned a little girl vainly attempting to explain how it must have fallen out of her pocket on the way home from school.

I pictured a mom fighting to maintain self-control, while she recalled spending two days struggling to knit one pair from some yarn she had been given. Store-bought mitts were just too expensive.

Memories surfaced of my own children who, by the end of winter, always seemed to have had an assortment of mismatched mitts.

My lips twisted into a wry smile as I thought of the times my mother made strings that passed through my coat sleeves and connected my knitted mittens.

Slowly, gently, I placed the tiny article on a nearby fence post, and wondered if its owner would discover it as easily as I had found my lost mitten memories.

Mister Bristles

A cursory glance at a local map stirred a long-forgotten memory.

Long before cars used Tennyson Road, we kids would bicycle down the long grassy trail to visit Mr. Bristles at his house by the lake.

We went there to listen to his many stories, which seemed to flow from his carved face and large hands.

Mr. Bristles wasn't his real name. We nicknamed him that due to the stiff hairs sticking out from his ears, his nose and his eyebrows. After a while all you noticed were shiny black eyes twinkling above the gentle smile.

His place was more shack than house. It was built from the bits-and-pieces gathered from around Bob Lake. In a way it was a perfect representation of his life and the continuous patchwork of stories coming from Mr. Bristles' past.

We were an eager audience, watching his old chipped pipe punctuating important points as the current adventure progressed.

My mom suggested I not bother the old man. "He's had a hard time, you know, and would probably like some peace and quiet."

When I asked her what she knew about Mr. Bristles, she ran her fingers through her hair. "I'm not sure. Nobody seems to know much about him. I heard that he was a sailor during World War One. Some say he is part Ojibwa. Folks should just leave him alone. You should too."

I'm glad I did not take her advice.

I have forgotten all the stories he told us except the legend of how the beaver stole fire from the gods, and gave it to humans.

Don't know why that particular story is etched in my head.

What I do recall is how Old Mr. Bristles always seemed to reflect something from his past back into our time. He made us think of how we should view life and each other.

Another thing he did was to show how Mother Nature — that's what he called the outdoors — is there for our enjoyment and health, as many ailments can be treated from certain trees and bushes.

I can't remember the names of all the medicinal plants he showed us and what they did. The one I do recall is from the day we were sitting around a small campfire — he always had one going — and trying to make birch bark baskets using spruce roots.

When I complained about having a headache, he made a tea by scraping the inside of a willow branch into some hot water.

"Here," he said,"Drink some of this a bit at a time."

It wasn't long until I felt better.

The visits became less frequent as high school and other interests occupied my life.

It was during second year of post-grad studies I learned about the passing of Mr. Bristles.

I wish I had learned his real name.

Another Delay

The setting sun forced me to squint at the new unfamiliar territory which was about to become home.

We were nearing the end of another long tedious day on the Oregon-Bozeman Trail. I could see Chimney Rock ahead.

In 1862, Congress passed The Homestead Act which gave 160 acres to anyone who stayed five years and improved the land, whereupon they could own the land and could purchase more at $1.25 an acre.

Our application in Nebraska had been successful.

According to the government map, our farm was edging a small river a week east of Scotts Bluff.

Another day or so and we should be there.

I smiled. My husband Henry, lulled by the uneven rocking of the wagon, and din of paraphernalia clanging against the sides, had nodded off while our team automatically followed the other covered wagons in the train.

As I glanced down and rubbed the spot where our first baby was kicking, the wagon came to a halt.

"Whoa team!" he called. "Look at that, Martha. Old George is up to his axles right in the middle of the crossing!"

Sure enough, the wagon in front was stuck in the river crossing mud.

I patted Henry's shoulder. "Now calm down, dear. It's just another delay. Maybe that rain last night changed the channel."

"Well, we can't just sit here", he fumed, "They only hold the homestead territories open for so long, you know."

"You're such a worrier. We have our signed papers, so there is nothing to panic about."

Henry sighed. "You're right as usual Martha. Well I don't like being half in and half out of the river like this. Maybe I can slip by him on the left."

"And get stuck yourself! Don't be silly. George is our friend. I grant you he is a bit rough around the edges, but he is not as cranky as you seem to think he is. Two days back, he helped the Corrigans with their broken wheel, and he did fix our leaking water barrel."

"He certainly is a good carpenter."

"And as long as he is stuck we, along with the rest of the train, are stalled."

Henry took a long swallow of water from the canteen, and then called, "Hang on George! I'll bring my team up there."

He handed me the canteen and then flashed one of his gorgeous smiles that had won my heart four years ago. "I shouldn't be too long, dear."

As Henry unhitched the team, I dampened a cloth from the flask, and wiped my face, neck and throat.

"I'll have dry clothes for you when you get back."

"Thank you dear; I'll see you in a few minutes."

The Value
of the Craftsman

To have my grandfather's pocket watch repaired I sought out a watchmaker who was recommended by several friends.

After cruising up and down the specified street I finally spotted the tiny repair shop crushed between its two modern neighbours.

As the sharp entrance-bell ting faded into the antique walls, an "I'll be right with you." greeted me from an old but well-lit worktable.

"No hurry," I answered. "Mind if I watch? Pardon the pun."

There was a small shrug.

The watchmaker's hands seemed as resilient and weather-beaten as the overhead sidewalk sign.

Beneath his unmoving monocle, wrinkled yet nimble fingers automatically retrieved the desired tool from an implement arrangement obviously established through the years.

My own fingers twitched as tapered tweezers manoeuvred petite cogs and wheels into predetermined positions where thread-thin screwdrivers secured them with almost-invisible screws.

Shaped into curves immaculate the fingernails were complementary additions to the miniature instruments.

I noticed that the first carpel joint of the middle finger had gained an extra 'wrinkle' where screwdrivers had eroded their own groove. *247*

Marked by the wall-clock persistent tick-tock, time became both poignant and irrelevant. I had entered an age when pride in workmanship was treasured; when an artisan's life was valued and recorded in the craftsmanship.

I knew Grandpa's watch would be in capable hands.

The Sweet Smell of Success

When Hudson Bay Mining and Smelting discovered gold some hundred miles east of FlinFlon, Manitoba, the little town of Snow Lake was carved out of the black spruce forest beside its namesake lake.

The isolated community of nine hundred proved to be a quiet safe place to raise families and to develop the strong long lasting friendships common among mining people.

Crime was nonexistent.

The work force ranged from the mainly Caucasian executives and foremen, to the immigrants that composed the bulk of the work force. Although these new-arrivals spoke very little English, the community eagerly adopted them. Soon Portuguese, Polish, and Slavic music blended into the various community holidays such as Christmas concerts.

Slipping in and out of town were the Northern Cree who renewed their supplies by exchanging furs at the Hudson's Bay Company. A small percentage of these trappers were amateur prospectors who brought samples to the mine to be assayed.

One particular prospector, Casper, was as weather-beaten as a solitary pine on a wind-swept island, and as ageless as the Canadian Shield he roamed.

Casper's stocky wrinkled frame was encased in the same scruffy coat and woollen-grey pants stuffed in his half-laced bush-boots. Equally-spaced around his warped brimmed black hat dangled numerous beads to ward off mosquitoes and black flies.

He had one distinguishing feature: a pockmarked half-golf-ball-sized growth on the end of his nose. I now know it was a slow growing benign tumour, but the anomaly must have been a constant embarrassment for him.

One day Casper discovered a massive copper and nickel deposit near Ward Lake about thirty miles west of town.

The mining company optioned his claim.

Casper immediately bought new clothes, a shiny new pickup, and then chartered a plane to Winnipeg where they operated on his nose.

Although the town rejoiced with him, it seemed to miss that Old Casper look.

An Aborted Dance

"What the hell are you doing?" I yelled at the stranger standing on a stump

The loop around his neck said it all.

I had discovered the man while I was walking my dog out behind my cottage.

"Leave me alone! I've nothing to live for. Everything is gone."

"Wanna tell me about it first?"

"The man stared. You wouldn't understand."

"I can try."

I sat on a fallen tree.

"Well, it all started last week at the company dance. I was dancing with darling...."

"You can dance? Wish I could; especially a waltz. All I do it one-two-one–two around the floor."

"A waltz is easy. You just go one-two-three; one-two-three."

"Fine for you to say: then there is the fox trot and the tango and the rumba. Girls expect you to know how to do them, you know."

"Yeah, well some of them. Most people like the waltz and..."

Suddenly the guy remembered what he was talking about.

"Anyway, I was dancing with my darling to the Tennessee Waltz..."

Oh. Oh. He's one of those that has to start from the beginning each time.

"Yeah that is nice one. Personally I like the Kentucky Waltz by the Osborne Brothers."

"Don't know that one."

"Who was playing it?"

A confused look flashed across his face. "I don't know. Some ten-piece band the company hired. Does it matter?"

"Not really. Always sounds better with a full orchestra."

I could tell the guy was relaxing a bit.

"Anyway, I was dancing with my darling to the Tennessee Waltz when this old friend I happened to meet."

"Yeah I guess so. We went to the same school but he was a year or so behind me. We were on the same basket ball team for a couple of years."

"Sports are great in high school; makes up for a lot of crap studies."

"Yeah, I know what you mean."

The man blinked. "Never mind that. I was dancing with my darling to the Tennessee Waltz when this old friend I happened to meet. I introduced him to my darling...."

"That was nice....the polite thing to do."

"Well I thought so...be the gentleman and all that."

I could see anger seething beneath the surface. I'd have to choose my words carefully.

"Good for you."

He glared. "I was dancing with my darling to the Tennessee Waltz when this old friend I happened to meet. I introduced him to my darling, and while they were dancing, my friend stole my sweetheart from me!"

Tears welled up in his eyes.

"Nice friend," I said. "With friends like that who needs....well you know."

The man teetered on the stump.

He took a deep breath and sighed. I was dancing with my darling to the Tennessee Waltz when this old friend I happened to meet. I introduced him to my darling, and while they were dancing, my friend stole my sweetheart from me! I remember the night and the Tennessee Waltz."

"Yeah, and I'll bet you're losing sleep too."

"I've hardly slept a wink since."

"Well, it's hard to sleep after something like that happens."

"Anyway, I was dancing with my darling to the Tennessee Waltz when this old friend I happened to meet. I introduced him to my darling, and while they were dancing, my friend stole my sweetheart from me! I remember the night and the Tennessee Waltz, now I know just how much I have lost."

"Well, yes granted; but what did you lose really?"

"Are you completely stupid? I was dancing with my darling to the Tennessee Waltz when this old friend I happened to meet. I introduced him to my darling, and while they were dancing, my friend stole my sweetheart from me! I remember the night and the Tennessee Waltz, now I know just how much I have lost. I lost my little darling the night they were playing the beautiful Tennessee Waltz!"

Desperation was setting in. His feet began to shift.

"We planned to get married and everything!"

"Yes. Yes, quite likely but think about it. She meets another guy and poof. What would your marriage have been like?"

The man stopped moving.

"You'd be looking over your shoulder all the time."

"Yeah!"

Resolve cemented his face.

He yanked off the noose and jumped down.

"Why should I kill myself over someone like that?"

"Good thinking. Let's go inside. Want a beer?"

A Memoir

Once upon a time, when I was around six years old, I put up a valiant effort to stay up late – or at least later.

Mom had put me to bed a long time ago, and even though it was way past my bedtime, I felt wide-awake. After all, I was six years old now and raring to go.

I had exhausted the usual delays such as the I-need-a-drink-of-water and the I-hafta-go-to-the-bathroom bit, so I resorted to going to my bedroom door and peeking out.

After several sessions of this, Mom - probably at her wits end - said, "What do you want to do?"

"I wanna go outside and play."

"Fine!"

I was excited.

In a matter of minutes I was dressed in my winter snowsuit and trundled outside.

Beyond the edge of the light from the kitchen window casting its meager light off the snow banks, loomed a dark forbidding world.

'Hey, wait a minute,' I thought. 'This was not what I had in mind.'

Suddenly a nice warm bed seemed much more appealing.

I banged on the window and yelled, "I wanna go to bed. I wanna go to bed!"

Finally, after what seemed like a very long time, I was let in.

I do not recall resisting the bedtime routine after that.

Canadian Hospitality

It was New Years Day, and my young family and I were in a convoy of about fifteen east-bound cars struggling through a north-shore snow storm on Highway 17 near Montreal River.

With the gas needle edging towards the 'E', I was looking forward to topping-up at a well-known refuelling stop that also had a small restaurant.

I wasn't the only one thinking 'gas' because, in unison, the entire convoy swung left up the small hill.

The gas station was closed.

Another driver and I approached a nearby mobile home where we hoped to be directed to the station's owner.

We were speaking to him!

When the proprietor saw the yard was full of cars and understood our situation, he gladly opened up.

While we took turns filling up, residents from other mobile homes brought food to the cafe. In a matter of minutes hot coffee and hot chocolate joined the impromptu buffet on the small counter.

No charge was implied or requested.

Mothers with young children welcomed the use of the washroom facilities.

We paid for the fuel and gladly donated generously towards the food and kindness.

Handshakes and hugs accompanied heart-felt greetings of 'Happy New Year'.

Half an hour or so later, we resumed our travels with full tanks, full tummies, and hearts full of warm Canadian hospitality.

Oops!

Jack dropped his keys.

"Oops!" he laughed.

As he scrambled up onto the railroad trestle he spotted a man out at the mid point.

"Don't come any closer; I'll jump."

"Okay. Mind if I watch?"

"You don't think I'll jump do you?"

"It's not up to me."

"Well, I will."

"Fine, but you should move a little bit over this way."

"So that you can grab me?"

"No, it's just that you'll be over the river. It will cleanup easier."

"You're gross! Don't you care?"

"I can't care if I don't know the circumstances."

The man did not answer.

Jack played with his keys. "Um before you take off so to speak, would you mind telling me why you want to end it all?"

"Life," the man snarled. "There is nothing left."

"I suppose that depends upon what you expected, what you wanted."

"All I wanted was a chance, a bit of hope."

"True, everyone needs some ho…."

"But she lied, and lied and kept lying."

"So there is a woman involved."

"Yes!"

"Yeah, there usually is."

"I knew she was playing around. I'd find little things changed when I got home from work. I work nights as a security guard. One time when I asked her point blank, she became hyper - screaming and yelling and everything."

"Me thinks she doth protest too much."

"What?"

"It's a line from Shakespeare's Macbeth."

"I don't know nothing about that. All I know is when I came home early this morning, there they were, the two of them."

"Oops! Not good."

"But I fixed them. They won't be double-dealing no one no more."

"I get the picture. Do the police know yet?"

"No, but they soon will."

"I suppose so."

"Then that'll be the end of me."

"Which is why you've come here."

"Yeah, better this than the chair."

"That drop should do it."

The man nodded.

Jack seized the moment. "Maybe you could plead temporary insanity."

"Maybe."

"You acted in an understandable jealous rage."

"Yeah."

"How about self-defence?"

"No, the guy was a lot smaller than me."

"Well, sometimes a jury is lenient especially when they understand the circumstances."

Jack took a cigarette from its package and lit it. "I'm going to quit one of these days. These things will kill yuh."

Jack offered one to the man.

The man hesitated.

Jack shrugged. "I'll put the pack right here and you can help yourself."

"Oh no, you'll try to grab my hand."

"Actually, the thought never crossed my mind. Tell you what: I'll toss the pack and you catch it."

"Okay."

The tossed cigarette pack sailed slightly off course.

The man reached for the passing pack, but with flailing arms, disappeared.

There was a soft thud.

Jack looked down.

"Oops!"

A Doctor's Diagnosis
and Cure

On Wednesday afternoon the front desk buzzed to say a patient was in Doctor Alice's second waiting room. When she entered, a stalwart mid-twenties man sat inside and pressed a bloody cloth on his left forearm and hand.

Upon removing the rag Alice's knees nearly buckled.

Her muddled mind searched for a fleeting memory.

She found it.

It was those tattoos.

Less than a year ago—in her home, in her shower—she'd been attacked. Her rapist had been ruthless; the knife at her throat made compliance absolute until he had finished with her. When it vanished she felt a pain in her skull, fell to the floor, and watched his boots while the beast fled out of her apartment.

She never saw enough of her attacker for the police to find him. All she remembered was those tattoos—a laughing skull with a red R over its cracked dome, perhaps an initial for the beast's name—on his forearm while he pumped her from behind—

Alice quickly closed the man's cut, calmer than she thought she'd be able.

"Are you allergic to any particular drugs?" she asked him, surprised at how steady the words came.

The man said he just had to watch out for wasps.

Leaving a nurse to finish dressing the wound, Alice went to record the man's treatment. Alice deliberately closed the new file without noting anything about her rape, or the man's allergy.

That night Alice found the wasp nest in her backyard. She slipped a plastic bag over it, and then put the nest in the freezer.

At three fifty-five, she hurried to the freezer where she gently tapped the bag. Satisfied the inhabitants were dead, she put the bag on the table and gingerly cut it open.

She snipped off each abdomen end and put them into the mortar. After grinding the stingers and adding distilled water, her filtered mixture yielded five millilitres of pale-yellow oily liquid which she transferred to a syringe.

On Thursday after work she put on her coat, slipped on a pair of sunglasses, tied a kerchief over her hair, and then followed her rapist onto the subway platform. It was easy to find him. He'd left his correct address.

The sound of wheels increased the crowd's jostling. With one smooth motion Alice injected the venom into the man's thigh, before she quickly moved away.

The man grabbed his leg. People backed away from his flailing arms. The man wheezed and clawed at his throat. Suddenly he staggered backwards and fell off the platform— just as the train roared into the station.

The screams, the squeal of brakes were simultaneous.

A news bulletin mentioned how a terrible accident had closed the Norwood station.

Alice called her boyfriend Brian. "Let's go to a fancy restaurant. My treat."

He asked, "What's the occasion?"

"Nothing spectacular," she answered with a smile. "I finally got rid of a wasp nest along with some other garbage. Now I feel like champagne."

Anticlimax

I felt alone and empty. Unresolved grief knotted my stomach.

It wasn't fair. Just when everything was coming together for Barry and his new family, my best friend had been killed in bazaar car crash.

Seeking solace, I had retreated to an isolated section of the park, where the squeals of children and adult laughter seemed to add 'salt' to my spiritual wounds.

Didn't they care? Didn't they know that one of the nicest fellows one could ever hope to meet was dead?

But how could they?

I was blankly staring between my feet - trying to make some sense of the tragedy – when an ant appeared. With her antennae rapidly surveying the area, she became focused on something straight ahead. I followed her gaze to a large cookie crumb lying in the middle of the sidewalk.

'What a prize.'

The ant took a few steps, hesitated, advanced some more, and then boldly stuck out for the morsel.

I cheered her on: 'Go, girl, go!'

She grasped the large crumb, turned, and headed back.

I whispered, 'Hurry up! Come on. Come on!'
A pair of legs strolled between us.
"No," I yelled!
The ant lay crushed beside her prize.
Wretchedness engulfed me.
I buried my face in my hands and cried for Barry ... and my ant.

The Pop Can

"And finally," **said** **Sergeant** **Thompson,** snapping the night-duty roster closed, "Benson, you and Burns make a couple of extra swings through the east end tonight. We have received several missing person reports from that area. See the dispatcher for the details."

"Yes, sir," answered Constable Benson, and then turned to his partner, "You know, we haven't seen Murphy and his friend Sam for quite a while."

Constable Burns nodded. "That's right. Come to think of it, we used to run into that one-armed guy once in a while - I think his name was Farley."

"Well, I guess we should sign out. I'm looking forward to another quiet night."

Meanwhile Willie Knight fretted as he shuffled along the dusty dimly-lit street. He had not seen Sam and Murphy for days.

"Farley will know where they are," he muttered out loud. "He's usually knocking around here somewhere."

Willie patted his shirt pocket, and then cursed when he remembered had bummed a cigarette from a guy at the Salvation Army Kitchen.

He tightened his scruffy coat, and headed for the bus stop where riders often threw away long butts.

A wind gust blew street-dust into his eyes. Upon clearing them, he noticed a shiny pop can sitting in the circle of light under the streetlamp.

His sneaker sent the container tumbling. The brash clatter shattered night. Willie smiled at his accomplishment, even if it was momentary and pitiful.

Although he hadn't kicked it that hard, his misty mind noticed the strange manner in which the dented can kept tumbling over and over until it came to rest upright just inside the opening of a dark but very narrow alleyway.

Willie scowled. Although he was quite familiar with 'his territory', his addled brain could not recall this particular passageway.

He peered into the cavern where a faint light shimmered at the far end.

It looked like a door.

Willie squeezed into the passageway. The brightness increased - almost beckoned - the further he ventured.

Eventually he faced the 'entrance'.

Willie figured it was a special door because it did not have a handle, or even hinges for that matter. In fact, the whole rectangle ebbed and flowed with deep blues, greens and purples slowly swirling around a pulsating inky core.

His neck hairs tingled.

Instinct cautioned him to leave things alone, but he just had to see what the door felt like.

Shaky dirty fingers reached out.

With a purple-green flash Willie vanished!

At that moment, the pop can regained its original shape, flopped over, and then rolled out under the street lamp where it sat up just as a patrol car cruised by. Twin spotlights scanned the shadows. One beam briefly probed the tiny alley and lingered on the can before moving away.

Later on that night Vinnie, The Merchant, Marconi shuffled along in the gloomy street. He was worried because had not seen Murphy and Farley for days.

"Willie will know where they are," he mumbled, "He'll be around here somewhere."

Dust from the road temporarily blinded him. When he could see again, he spotted a pop can sitting in the circle of light cast by the streetlamp.

Vinnie kicked it, but noticed the strange manner in which the container bounced over and over until it stood upright at the opening of a narrow dark alley.

A strange light emanated at the far end.

It looked like a door.

He just had to see what that light was.

The Defense Rests

It will be great to see Steven again. I'm glad his sister called. – She sounded worried. - Wouldn't tell me why he was in the hospital. - This box of chocolates should brighten his spirits. – He always did have a sweet tooth especially when he played hockey. – Very few ever got past his defensive position. – Could play the whole game and never tire out. – Would have been a terrific role model for the kids except for his chain-smoking habit. – I wonder what he has been doing these past years.

Hospitals always smell the same. – Antiseptic and cleaning fluid, formaldehyde and death. – It's certainly not a place one willingly visits. – Ah, there's the front desk.

Hi there, how'er you doing? – I've come to visit a Mr. Steven Spencer. – Supposed to have been registered here about a week ago. – Would you tell me what room he is in? – I've brought him some chocolates. – They should perk him up eh? – Fifth floor the 'C'-Wing, number 523? – Elevator's over there? Thank you.

I hope he won't be disappointed I didn't bring him any of his cigarettes. – He and that Philip Morris pack were never apart. – He was always ready to show the detail saying they were 'Scientifically proven far less irritating to the smoker's nose and throat'. - Well, knowing Steve, as soon as he is fixed up, he will be back on the ice.

Here we are. - Push the fifth-floor button aaaaaaaand ta-da I here am.

My god what dreary atmosphere! – There's the nurses' station. – Good morning. – I'm here to see a Mr. Spencer in 523. – I'm an old school chum. – We played hockey together. - I've brought him some chocolates. – Steven is crazy for... – Leave them here? – Special diet I suppose eh? – Well may I visit him anyway? – Don't stay too long? - Okay I won't. – Down this way? – Thank you.

519 – 521- 523 – Good heavens, the room is a sterilized machine shop! – I recognize some of the humming devices. - That is an aspirator tube draining his chest. – The heart line rate on the monitor looks pretty good. – Oh my, he's had a tracheotomy. - No wonder the nurse suggested I leave the chocolates. - This isn't the Steven I knew. – He is half the size he was! – His hand is a bunch of ice-bones. – Hey Steven, it's me George! – I've come to see how you are doing. – Good, he squeezed my hand. – He knows it's me. - Yeah it's me Steven your old left winger. - You can't play hockey like this! - Is there anything you want? - Can I get you anything? - Oh God, break my heart. - He's holding up two fingers, two nicotine stained fingers.

I think I'm going to be sick.

When I am King of the World I Will...

No, no, I don't think I'll do that.

Well, when I am King of the World, I will collect the greatest minds together, and have them create an odourless tasteless solution which when ingested, will bring everyone's mind into a oneness of thought and direction.

Come to think of it, that won't work because with identical thinking there would be no creativeness.

Okay then, I'll change the solution's formula so that it makes everyone speak the same language. Everyone will argue in the same tongue, which should exacerbate problems to the point that no one will speak to each other.

Hm, not good.

Well then, when I am King of the World, I shall have the scientists create a solution that will make everyone tell the truth.

Hm, I've heard this can cause problems because not everyone wants to hear the whole truth. A good example of this is the American people and the Iraq War fiasco.

But, I digress.

Well then, when I am King of the World, there will be no pollution. That should improve things.

Come to think of it, I would have to eliminate cars, trucks, diesel engines, smoke-producing factories, and most industries! The place would be a maze of paved roads winding between nonfunctioning buildings!

With a bit of extrapolation, people would become more fit because they will have to ride bicycles, walk or resort to horses.

Hm, the horses might present a bit of a problem. No doubt some whiney environmentalists will make a fuss, so I will designate them as official scoopers.

Okay, well when I am King of the World all lawyers and judges will be forced to become farmers where, after a few years of honest work, they will learn reality. Upon returning to society they will have more realistic view of life and crime.

Speaking of crime, murderers, rapists, child pornographers and drug pushers will be eliminated. If a judge decides to let a killer out on bail, that judge will face the same wall.

I will have specially designed jails built in the tundra regions.

A point of interest: In the tundra region, it has been estimated that the total weight of the mosquito population is several times more than the total mass of the caribou herds.

These jails will have roofs, walls, floors, and the barest of sleeping accommodations and be sectioned off into three areas.

One section has normal living conditions, as far as jails go, but the main pleasantry will be the access to insect repellant.

The second section is for those who have misbehaved and treated their fellow citizens badly. They must live where there are some holes conveniently left open for the mosquitoes.

The third section is for con men, CEO's who steal from their clients, wife abusers, gangsters, thieves, and the like, including more lawyers. These buildings will have no screens allowing the millions of mosquitoes to gradually slowly inexorably drain the inmates dry.

The very thought of being locked in such a place should keep most people on the straight and narrow.

With such delicious thoughts playing on my mind, I really should turn my attention to the water situation in large urban areas, but I'll save that for another day.

Right now I see nurse coming with my pills, but if I push hard on this thick padded door she won't get in. Then she'll have to get someone to help her and then.......

A Pond Farewell

Oops! Excuse me, sir or madam frog, I didn't mean to startle you by dropping my empty pill container. I just came to spend a few lingering minutes beside your pond.

I'll bet that cool water was a bit of a shock after becoming so nice and warm in the sun, eh?

I knew where you were because, when your eyes broke the surface, they caused tiny concentric circles to ripple out from your position.

I won't bother you. Climb back upon your dry rock and together we will contemplate the meaning of life as reflected in your pond.

Gorgeous day, isn't it? I just came here to enjoy a last few moments of peace before...before escaping to...whatever.

Your existence here must be a damn sight easier than what we humans have to endure.

You don't believe me? Consider those whirligigs. Watch how they meander and glide within an unspecified boundary, their double-lenses searching above and below the

waterline as if attempting to see two worlds at once.

Yet, if one or two become excited, the rest scatter, frenetically diving or spinning around until things calm down.

I wonder if they ever find out who started the commotion.

It is the same with human teenagers with their fads and music. Even university students become fanatical about inane situations. How do you think wars start? Sometimes saner heads prevail, but not often.

Watch that colourful undulating leech slowly cruising above the pebbles as it searches for prey. Once he and his cousin, the lamprey, latch on, there is no escape.

In my world they are called pimps, drug pushers, and bankers who suck everything out of people. Nothing is left. Nothing! Not even the will to live.

I can see some tiny fish fry skittering among the thin grass. If it weren't for those thin weeds gently swaying in one direction, you would never know there was a current here.

It is the same in the human world. Different types of subtle undercurrents pervade all societies. The people exist, struggle within it, mature and hopefully find their own way.

Many don't make it.

You might say that snail represents a persistent person who steadily — resolutely — makes his own course through life, constantly progressing along upon a path of his own creation. And, due to receiving several hard knocks all through life, he or she builds a shell around himself or herself to prevent — with any luck - further injury.

It doesn't always work.

Consider how that erratic water strider, with its hairy feet allowing it scamper across the water without breaking the surface tension, uses its rapier mouth to pounce upon vulnerable creatures and suck them dry.

Did you know there are humans like that? They lurk about

on the fringes of society, picking off their fellow beings, and draining them physically, financially, or worse spiritually dry?

Lawyers are a good example.

That scuttling crawfish is also looking for weak or injured creatures, just like the predators that lurk around bus stations, watching for the teenagers who are 'run-aways'.

It is the same in the human world. If a person is fortunate enough to escape one menace, another more deadly one is lying in wait.

I should know.

Watch that leaf floating in this direction. In a way, it could represent a person's life adventure: spinning off small snags, becoming stuck briefly, but then moving on to an unknown destination.

But some leaves never get free. Never! No matter how they struggle, they are tossed around until they are completely used up; after which they are discarded, alone and empty upon the river of destiny.

Speaking of fate, I hope you don't think I'm impolite, but I am becoming very sleepy. I think I'll lay back here and listen to the forest sounds and....

Ancient History Revisited

Fox was restless. It was one of those dull drizzly days when every tree branch and grass blade instantly soaked the fur, thus deterring outdoor activities.

He tried dozing, hoping the skies would clear to let the moon allow for a bit of hunting. Right now the inactivity was really starting to irritate him.

As Fox's eyes strayed across the bookshelf, one faded ratty spine entitled THE BOOK OF WILES sparked his interest.

"Hummm, it has been a long time since I have consulted that book. Maybe I should brush up on a few things."

After depositing the rather thick volume on the table, he brewed a pot of tea, turned on the light, and pushed back in his recliner.

When he scanned the table of contents he noticed a small asterisk beside the topic: CHASES. At the bottom of the page the starred notation read: Void in cases of the G.B.M. (See Appendix).

Fox thumbed to the back where he found the desired discussion as an addendum in Appendix VI entitled Lessons Learned: From the Diary of Ferdinand Fox.

Under this entry he found Chase Variations Involving G.B.M.

'It must be understood that, although any chase is conducted with full concentrated intensity, keeping in mind the logical outcome from such a large expenditure of energy, (which of course must be determined prior to any pursuit), this criteria does not hold true in cases involving the G.B.M., aka: The Ginger Bread Man. (See Glossary)'

Fox flipped back to the Table of Contents, located the Glossary, and then frenziedly found Ginger Bread Man.

'GINGER BREAD MAN: A mystical biscuit boy who appears periodically to old couples who cannot have – but truly desire - children.

Once created this exceptionally fast cookie-child invariably runs away, and uses the taunting irritating refrain:

"Run, run, as fast as you can.

You can't catch me!

I'm The Ginger Bread Man."

This results in a long line of exhausted people and animals running across the countryside.'

Fox could hardly wait to return to Chase Variations.

. . . .

The following procedure has proven effective.

THE G.B.M PROCEDURE

Should the G.B.M. be encountered, under no circumstances is a chase to be initiated.

The G.B.M. is extremely quick and particularly manoeu-vrable. Any effort to seize him is futile.

(See Chase Criteria)

You must make him come to you.

It is essential that disinterest be feigned.

Be discourteous and rude.

Instruct him to cease the refrain.

Tell the G.B.M. to leave you alone. This will infuriate him and he will become curious.

It is this curiosity that makes him vulnerable.

Since encounters consistently occur by rivers, the G.B.M. will ask to be taken across.

DO NOT TAKE HIM ACROSS, at least not right away.

Create excuses. (Use own imagination here).

Delay the crossing until you hear the country folk coming.

The noise of their approach will cause the G.B.M. to suppress his timidity.

Invite the G.B.M. to climb onto your back.

Gently enter the water so that your back stays dry...for a while.

As you progress, slowly sink further causing the water to inch up onto your back, thus forcing the G.B.M. to climb onto your shoulders.

Gradually ensure your fur absorbs enough water so the G.B.M. will be relegated to the top of your head.

When the G.B.M is comfortable, flip your head back to toss him into the air where you can easily catch and gobble him down.

(Essential directive).

Rinse your mouth thoroughly.

Once back on shore, deny any knowledge of a Ginger Bread Man.'

Fox shut the book, sank into the cushions and closed his eyes to absorb the new information.

He nodded off.

Upon awakening he could hear birds singing.

The Fox stretched, scratched, and then ventured out to his lookout rock from where he saw a strange ragged procession scrambling along the fence line on the far side of the farm.

Although he knew the wind often sang through the trees, he was puzzled by a melody: "Run, run, as fast as you can...."

Lakeside
Departure – #2

Harold's arm trembled as his trusty cane helped him along the sidewalk. At his age, it was normal to be tired, but this particular morning, he was downright plumb tuckered out.

The tight-ache in his chest did not help.

He had forced himself out of bed and had hustled to the park to maintain his self-imposed schedule of sitting by the pond from late morning until well into evening. Harold enjoyed watching the ducks, geese, and swans. He also liked observing park visitors absorbed in their respective worlds.

Harold berated himself for rushing so, but rationalized that people expected him to be there, there on Harold's Throne. It wasn't really 'his bench', but through the years there was an unspoken understanding that the seat was reserved for Harold.

A shaking hand clasped the park bench as, gasping and wheezing, he eased himself onto his bench; the one nearest the fountain; the one at the intersection of several paths.

Many folks engaged him in conversations ranging from astrophysics to farming, from genetics to geography. Often the philosophical discussions he motivated made people late for work. They would laugh and hurry off, vowing to return tomorrow to continue the debate.

He had not eaten breakfast, but that was okay. Pete and his food cart would soon be along. Lately Pete refused payment saying it was 'his treat'. Harold insisted upon paying for the ice cream bar. In the evening it was the same routine.

Another constant in Harold's life was the Mounted Police Patrol team of Constable Laurie McPherson and Constable James McKinnon who usually spent a few minutes with him while their horses drank at the fountain. If it was late in the evening, they would escort him home.

Many major dialogues occurred at lunchtime when people shared their lives as well as their lunches. He became their confidant, their counsellor, and their grandpa.

Although he never told anyone what to do, he tactfully steered anxious individuals onto corrective courses.

Often, with his heart aching from numerous histories, Harold fretted all night, and hoped to meet the same individuals again.

This day should have followed the same pattern, but Harold became increasingly edgy and irritated. He found it difficult to maintain a coherent conversation. People arrived with eager smiles, only to excuse themselves, and leave with quizzical looks.

Asked if he was all right Harold, with a wave of his bony hand and a frail almost-toothless smile, assured them he was just very tired today.

He was surprised when the park lights came on. Although it was late, he reasoned that he would head home when the heavy tightness eased up.

He stared across the pond. Some ducks sliced through the moon's reflection.

A weak smile glimmered. "What a perfect way to end the day."

He took a deep breath and hoped a short nap would help.

After a shuddering sigh his chin rested on his chest.

He did not hear the clip-clop of horses that stopped in front of him.

He did not see the tears in Laurie McPherson's eyes.

He did not hear Constable McKinnon call the coroner's office.

Harold had left the park.

Biographical Note

J. Graham Ducker is an Oshawa resident, a published author, a poet, retired Principal, Primary Methods Specialist and former Kindergarten Teacher.

Mr. Ducker has received National and International awards and recognition for his writing. He had the esteemed title of being the Poet Laureate of Oshawa for 5 years.

His published memoir book entitled, *Don't Wake the Teacher,* is an integral part of the University of Holguin Teachers College.

He has had two poetry books published: *Observations of the Heart and Mind*, and *Where Warm Hearts Blend.*

Some of Graham Ducker's Awards

– The Short story, **"Life in a Leaf"**, placed first in the *Mariposa Literary Contest 2008*.

– The short story, **"A Culinary Connection"**, placed third in the *Mariposa Literary Contest 2009*.

– The short story, **"Long Ago and Far Away"**, received first place standing in the *Lichen Epistolary Fiction 2006*.

– The poem "**Thirty-Three**" received third prize in *BLUSH II Magazine Poetry Contest*, published by the *Uxbridge Times/ Journal, Spring 2001*.

– The short story **"Ship Building"** received an Honourable Mention in the *72nd* *Annual Writer's Digest Writing Competition*.

– The re-entered short story **"Ship Repairs"** received another Honourable Mention in the *74th* *Writer's Digest Writing Competition* out of **18,000 entries**.